Martin Berry

GLOW WORMS

When young Jack makes a mysterious discovery
in an old well, he soon finds himself in a strange
alliance with an alien visitor

Mereo Books

2nd Floor, 6-8 Dyer Street, Cirencester, Gloucestershire, GL7 2PF
An imprint of Memoirs Book Ltd. www.mereobooks.com

Glow worms: 978-1-86151-956-6

First published in Great Britain in 2019
by Mereo Books, an imprint of Memoirs Books Ltd.

Copyright ©2019

Martin Berry has asserted his right under the Copyright Designs and Patents
Act 1988 to be identified as the author of this work.

The address for Memoirs Books Ltd. can be
found at www.memoirspublishing.com

Memoirs Books Ltd. Reg. No. 7834348

Typeset in 13/20pt Century Schoolbook
by Wiltshire Associates Ltd.
Printed and bound in Great Britain

1

Jack knew, the moment he'd thrown the frisbee, that he'd made a mess of it. It veered off at an angle, flying towards the house. It smacked the back wall, narrowly missing the upstairs landing window, dropped down on the lean-to roof, and continued its chaotic journey, clattering across the glass roof before finally falling down inside through a skylight.

Jack breathed a sigh of relief. He'd been lucky. It hadn't broken anything. But his relief was short lived, as a moment later there was a loud crash, and a large hole appeared in a glass pane at the front.

He ran across the lawn to the door at the far end. The sight inside filled him with dismay. There were plant pots on their sides everywhere he looked, and the dirt from them was scattered across the quarry-tiled floor. Cody, his black Labrador, was in the middle of it all, nosing around for his Frisbee, wagging his tail enthusiastically.

There was broken glass on the floor, so Jack grabbed hold of Cody's collar and dragged him over to the door. Jack was small for his age, but also wiry and strong, and as he pulled the dog towards the door, his lopsided fringe of mousy brown hair kept falling down over his left eye.

He had just managed to get Cody outside when someone called out to him.

"Jack? Jack! What's going on?"

He turned to see his aunt steaming across the lawn towards him, her cheeks red and puffed up as if she were about to explode. For a large woman, she was quick on her feet, and she was upon him in no time.

"Did you do that?" shouted Aunt Lori, pointing to the broken pane at the front of the lean-to.

"Eh... no," said Jack, trying to look and sound as innocent as possible.

"So it had nothing to do with that frisbee I saw you throwing a minute ago," said Aunt Lori.

"No, I don't think so."

"Follow me, Jack BURROWS!" she barked, and marched towards the door.

The lean-to ran along the back of the house. Knocked together from old wooden window frames, it was part greenhouse, part conservatory, and there was a small seating area with two wicker chairs and a round cast iron table amongst the taller plants at one end.

Aunt Lori frowned as she looked around at the mess inside. "Oh no, not my lemon tree!" she cried. She picked up a bright green flower-pot at the side of the door and carefully stood it back onto its base, then looked through the leaves of the small tree it contained. "The lemon's fallen off," she exclaimed. "That's the first one I've managed to grow." She saw it on the floor, and picked it up.

Jack couldn't see what all the fuss was about, as the lemon was only the size of a large grape, but he didn't say anything because he knew how fond his aunt was of her plants. She put the tiny lemon on a shelf next to the door, and then made her way over to the hole in the windowpane at the conservatory end of the lean-to.

An oak plant stand was lying on its side in front of the hole, with a dark blue flower-pot nearby. The pot was cracked in two, and a plant with spectacular white flowers and an exposed root ball was sitting between the two halves.

She looked up and glared across at him. "You keep that damn dog out of here in future, do you hear?"

Jack nodded sheepishly.

"Pick up those tomatoes!" she snapped,

pointing to a narrow bed at the front with several plants tied to bamboo canes. "At least they won't go to waste."

Jack knew he would have to get away before his aunt found him another job to do. After picking up the last tomato and placing it on the side with the others, he inched his way over to the door. Then, facing Aunt Lori, who was busy kneeling down scooping the lily into another pot, he started making pincer movements behind his back – a bit like a sock puppet talking. Right on cue, Cody, who was sitting outside, started barking.

Aunt Lori looked up. "Now where's that dustpan? I only used it the other... Oh, do take that dog away, I can't think with all that noise."

It never fails, thought Jack, making a hasty exit out of the door and setting off down the garden. "Come on Cody, let's go and see what Uncle Fred's up to."

Jack had been getting a scolding from his aunt the first time he had discovered this trick. They had been in the kitchen and Ryan Gainer, his best friend, had been standing behind him. Jack had made the hand gesture to mimic her going on and on at him. It had come as quite a shock when Cody barked, because he was usually pretty quiet indoors. Jack realised that it was the pincer movements he was doing with his hand that made Cody bark, and he'd been using the same dodge to get himself out of tight spots ever since.

Jack's parents had both died in a car accident a few years before, when Jack, an only child, was six years old. He had been staying in Port Marron for a short holiday, and they had been driving down to take him back home to London. The night they travelled down there was a torrential thunderstorm, and their car had skidded off the road down a steep embankment and crashed into a tree.

After the accident Aunt Lori and Uncle Fred had adopted Jack, and found Cody for him. They didn't have children of their own and thought a dog would be company for him. They were right about that.

2

As he walked down the garden path, Jack
could see the Jolly Roger waving at the top of
the pole at the end of Uncle Fred's workshop.
Flying the Skull and Crossbones when he
was in the workshop was one of Uncle Fred's
little jokes. He had only two flags, the other
being the Cornish flag, which he flew on Saint
Piran's day. The flags had originally been
raised and lowered by hand, but they were
now powered by an electric motor located
inside a wooden box at the bottom. The
flagpole had been converted some time ago,

and the gears coupled to the motor were in urgent need of lubrication, so they squeaked loudly in protest each time the motor was operated.

Uncle Fred had once been the skipper and owner of a small fishing boat called *Blue Angel*, and Jack occasionally sailed with him and helped out on board. But three years ago, whilst out in high seas, Uncle Fred had slipped on deck, fallen awkwardly and injured his leg. He had been advised by his doctor to give up fishing, so he reluctantly sold the *Blue Angel* and the business to Cadan, one of the crew. Over the months that followed his leg had slowly improved, so he could still get around, but he now walked with an obvious limp.

It wasn't safe for Cody inside the workshop, as there were too many things he could hurt himself on. Jack turned towards him, raising his hand. "Stay!" he said firmly.

Cody grudgingly sank down on his haunches at the edge of the path.

Jack walked around to the door at the side

and did his special knock, two slow knocks followed by three quick ones: *Knock... knock... knock knock knock*.

Uncle Fred hollered from inside, "Who is it?"

As usual, Jack thought this was a silly question, because he was the only one who knew the knock.

"It's me, Jack."

Uncle Fred opened the door. He was dressed in old corduroy trousers and a holed navy-blue jumper. He was quite tall, so the thinning fly-away grey hair on the top of his head was brushing the small blue flowers of the climbing plant hanging down over the door. Since his accident he spent a lot of time in his workshop making things, things that no one else had thought of – he was a sort of inventor. The things he dreamt up were pretty weird, and Jack often wondered if maybe the reason no-one else had thought of them was that most of them didn't appear to be very useful.

Uncle Fred squinted down at Jack. His eyesight wasn't too good, but he refused to wear glasses.

"Ah, Jack. You're just in time to see my... well, come and see."

The workshop was an amazing place. It had a wide bench down the middle with a chunky vice at one end, which always seemed to have something clamped in it, whether it was being worked on or not. Uncle Fred didn't believe in tidying up, so the bench was always covered in lumps of material left over after cutting, along with various tools and other clutter. Fixed to the wall at the side of the door was a tool board with nails and hooks, it was painted with blue shadows, each the same shape as one of the tools, so it was easy to see where each one belonged. The board was just an arm's length from the bench, but the tools never seemed to make it that far, so most of the shadows of hammers, spanners, screwdrivers, saws and an assortment of other tools remained empty.

Failed inventions were everywhere. The larger ones were sitting on the floor, making it a hazardous place to walk. Few were still in one piece, because when Uncle Fred lost interest in one invention, which happened quite quickly, he would steal bits from it to build another.

He picked up a black umbrella from the bench. "I think this is the ONE, Jack," he said enthusiastically, his eyes gleaming. Calling something 'the ONE' meant Uncle Fred thought this was the invention that was going to make them rich. Jack noticed he had a contraption with two metal rings strapped around the top of his right arm.

"We'd better go outside for the next bit. We don't want to open this in here, it's bad luck," said Uncle Fred.

Outside, it came as no surprise to Jack to find that Cody had wandered off.

Uncle Fred moved to the middle of the path, and then waved the umbrella. "Now, imagine it's started to rain. You have your hands full

– maybe you're carrying some shopping. You need to shelter under your umbrella. But you can't, because you can't hold it up and carry the shopping at the same time. Well," he said grandly, "now you can!"

He pressed the button on the side of the umbrella and it flew open. "And now, the clever bit."

Taking the umbrella, he clipped the handle on to the strange contraption on his arm. When he took his hand away, the umbrella stayed upright. In fact, it was perfectly placed above his head, ready to shelter him from the rain. And, what's more, he now had both hands free. Jack was totally amazed; his uncle had actually invented something that worked.

"It's brilliant!" said Jack enthusiastically, raising his right hand. "High five!"

Uncle Fred raised his right hand to meet Jack's. But as he did so, the umbrella flipped over and whacked him on the head.

"Ow! I think it needs a bit more work," he

said, rubbing the top of his head. He looked somewhat perplexed that his invention had attacked him.

Jack had heard his uncle say that before. "Oh well – it nearly worked," he said, trying to sound upbeat about it.

"Mmm," said Uncle Fred, not sounding quite so sure. He unclipped the umbrella from his arm and folded it up. "Anyway, never mind that. I was thinking of running up the Zapper again. Do you fancy giving me a hand?"

"Yeah!" said Jack eagerly. To him, the Zapper was one of the best things ever. Uncle Fred had seen a picture of it in an old book whilst browsing in a second-hand shop in town. Its official name was a Van de Graaff Generator, and it was a machine for generating bolts of static electricity, like lightning, between two metal spheres. It had been really hot the day they had powered it up for the first time, so they had opened all the windows and propped open the door to let in some air. A giant bluebottle had flown in through the side window, landed on one of the spheres, and been zapped by a bolt of electricity. Jack had named the new machine 'the Zapper', and the name had stuck.

Uncle Fred had never been one for just copying things. He always liked to try and improve them, and he had made his machine much bigger than the one shown in the book. Sitting at the far end of the bench, it towered over Jack.

Jack reached up and took hold of the old sheet that was used to keep off the dust.

"That's it," said Uncle Fred, holding on to the sheet at the other side of the bench. "Now lift it – gently now."

As they lifted off the sheet, the silver sphere on top of the Zapper caught the light coming through the side window. It was as big as a football, and had a hole at the bottom, which fitted over the top of a clear plastic tube that rose up vertically from the base. There was a rubber belt running down the middle of the tube, which went around rollers at the top and bottom, the one at the bottom being turned by a motor. A smaller sphere was fixed to the end of a hand-held rod. A wire ran from this sphere to the base of the machine. The original motor had been too small to turn the belt sufficiently fast, so Uncle Fred had ordered a bigger, more powerful one, and now he had finally got around to fitting it.

Jack looked it over. "Is it all fixed again now?"

"Yes, that's the new motor there," said Uncle Fred, pointing to a shiny dark blue box at the bottom of the tube. "It should really fly now. I'll just get the battery."

To save on batteries, the Zapper was run from the same one that was used to run the flagpole. He returned moments later carrying it carefully, his fingers wrapped around underneath. He set it down inside a rectangular frame made from four strips of wood attached to the base of the Zapper. Then, after securing it in place with a leather belt, he took the two leads from the control box, one red and one black, each with a large crocodile clip at the end, and connected them to it.

"Right, stand back," said Uncle Fred. He leant over and flicked the switch on the control box to 'ON', and the new motor whirred into life. The belt inside the tube quickly spun to a blur. He picked up the plastic rod, and tentatively moved the small sphere at the far end towards the sphere on top. When it was a couple of inches away, a small bolt of electricity jumped across between the spheres, making a faint crackle.

He let several more bolts jump across, and then flicked the switch to 'OFF'.

"They weren't very big, I'll give it a tweak," he said.

Picking up a small screwdriver, he inserted it into a hole in the top of the speed control box sitting at the rear of the motor and turned it clockwise. "There, that should do it."

He flicked the power on again and the motor speeded up. It was turning much faster than before, and making a faint whine. Jack could feel the hair on his arms lifting as the air around the Zapper quickly became charged. The speed of the motor continued to climb, the whine becoming higher pitched, and much louder. There were a number of crackles. Uncle Fred edged forward, holding the rod out in front of him. When the small sphere was an arm's length away from the sphere on top, there was an ear-splitting crack and an enormous bright white bolt of electricity leapt across between the two, making both of them jump. More giant bolts followed, flying across the huge gap between the spheres, each one crackling fiercely and lighting up the workshop like the flash on a dozen cameras all going off at once. The speed of the motor was still climbing.

Uncle Fred frowned and beckoned Jack over. "Something's not right," he shouted above the whine and crackling that filled the air around them. "We need to turn it off." He passed the plastic rod over to Jack. "You keep attracting the bolts away from me, and I'll see if I can get to the switch."

Jack tentatively moved the sphere towards the sphere on top. A giant bolt leapt across and the handle shook. Then another and another, with hardly a pause in between. The air was fizzing around him, and he could feel his skin tingling. Uncle Fred picked up a wooden pole leaning against the wall. Then, crouching low and holding the pole out in front of him, he moved cautiously towards the Zapper. He reached towards the power switch, and tried to push it over. But each time he tried the switch moved slightly, and the pole slipped off. He tried again, and then again. Eventually, after several more frustrating attempts, he managed to push the switch to off. The power to the motor was cut, and it slowed down and came to a standstill.

Uncle Fred stood up and wiped the sweat from his forehead with the back of his hand. "Phew. Did you see those bolts? They were massive. I think I overdid it a bit there. We'll leave the dust cover off, it will remind me to take a look at it."

"Oh, okay," said Jack, a slight wobble in his voice. He'd been a bit too close to those massive bolts for his liking.

3

After lunch Uncle Fred and Aunt Lori drove to Kinley to do the weekly shop. They had asked Jack if he wanted to go with them, but he'd said he'd stay behind and look after Cody. The house was quiet, and he was sitting at the desk in his bedroom, working on a half-assembled model of a Lancaster Bomber. Model planes were sitting in rows on shelves in front of him, poised as if ready to take off.

The first model he'd built had been a Sopwith Camel, a small biplane, which sat at the far end of the upper shelf. He had seen it in a model shop, and thought the name sounded funny. Uncle Fred had bought it for him as a surprise present for his eighth birthday. When he looked at it now, he could see the finish wasn't as good as his more recent models. Surplus glue was bulging out down the joins, and he could see drips of paint running down the fuselage. It had been one of the simpler models with just twenty parts. He had come a long way since then, the models increasing in size and becoming more difficult to assemble. The Lancaster kit he was working on contained over two hundred parts.

As he was applying a bead of glue around one half of a tail fin, he noticed that the bottle was almost empty. He held the two halves together while they glued, then put them down on the desk and pulled opened a drawer to see if he could find more glue. He came across a half-used bottle at the back of the drawer, but when he squeezed it, he found it had gone hard. That was a nuisance.

He really wanted to finish the glueing so that he could make a start on the painting, which was the bit he enjoyed the most.

He walked over to the bed, sat down on it and shuffled up against the headboard, then checked his phone to see if he had any messages. Ryan was away. He had gone camping with his father, and Jack wanted to know when he would be back. Ryan's parents had split up, so he now lived with his mother, his father having moved out of the area, which meant he only saw him on alternate weekends and for the occasional short holiday.

There were no new messages from Ryan. Jack slid the phone back into his pocket, then stretched up and grabbed a handful of comics from the shelf above his head. As he pulled them down, he felt something land softly in his hair. He tipped his head forward, and a tiny red propeller fell into his lap. It was one of the propellers from his quadcopter.

He turned around and knelt on his pillow

to look for it. The comics were stacked up in a large untidy pile, and he found the quadcopter at the back of the pile, on its end, squashed up against the wall. He brought it and its equally small controller down from the shelf. Apart from the missing propeller, the tiny craft appeared to be in good shape. He carefully pushed the propeller back onto the shaft of the motor.

The quadcopter hadn't been used for some time, and he wasn't sure if it would charge up, but after a few minutes the light on the charger changed from red to green, and it was ready to go. Being so small, it was easily blown around by the wind, so he usually only flew it indoors. But it was more fun outside, if the weather was right.

He peered out of the window. It was dry, and the tops of the two tall conifers halfway down the garden at the back of the rockery were barely moving, so there was hardly any wind. It was perfect.

Leaving Cody snoring contentedly in his

basket in the corner, he went downstairs and out into the garden. Standing in the middle of the lawn, he slid the switch on the quadcopter to 'ON' and its blue and red lights started to flash. Then, holding it in his right hand and the controller in his left, he eased the joystick forward and the tiny craft took to the air. It looked so much smaller outdoors, buzzing away like an angry wasp.

He gently pushed on the joystick and sent it off down the garden. If it went too far, it would stop responding to the controller, so when it was over the rockery, he moved the controls to bring it back. The tiny copter responded, swinging around to face him.

As it was flying back towards him there was a freak gust of wind, which blew it sideways, and it disappeared behind the conifers. Jack killed the power and headed down the garden to look for it. He thought that by the direction it was heading it would probably have come down somewhere on the patio, behind the conifers.

The patio was the oldest part of the garden. Surrounded by a low wall, it was shaped like a figure of eight, the two rounded sections overlapping in the middle. There was a small statuette in the middle of one part and an old disused well in the middle of the other. Jack walked over and peered down the well. Even though it was a bright and sunny day he could only see a little way down; the rest of the well was swallowed up by the dark.

"Nope, not in there," he muttered to himself.

As he turned around, he saw a flash high up in the conifers. He moved across to the other side of the patio to get a better look. The tiny craft was wedged high up amongst the leaves of one the trees. He would need something to prod it down with. He remembered seeing some bamboo canes behind the workshop. Picking the longest one he could find, he took it back to the patio. Then he stood in front of the conifer, stretching up and holding the cane high above his head. It was too short.

He looked around for something to give him

a bit more height. There was an old wooden bench facing the well, so he took hold of one of the arms and hauled it across the patio, then stepped up on to it and tried again. The end of the cane was now tantalisingly close, just inches below the branch the quadcopter was perched on. He just needed a little more height.

He moved one foot up on to the arm and shifted his other foot up on to the back, straddling the corner of the bench. As he gingerly straightened up, the bench creaked. Success! The end touched the quadcopter, and it moved.

He was about to prod it again when his phone rang. He dropped the cane and pulled it out from his pocket.

"Hell..."

As he spoke the arm of the bench gave way with a sharp crack, sending him toppling backwards through the air. He fell on to the bench, hitting his head, then rolled off it on to the ground.

For a moment he lay there, stunned and dazed by the fall. In a while his head began to clear, so he got up, pulled a handkerchief from one of the pockets of his jeans and dabbed the back of his head, examining it for signs of blood. It didn't seem to be bleeding.

As he was shoving the handkerchief back into his pocket, he realised he didn't have his phone. He looked around the bench. *That's crazy, where's that gone?*

At that moment someone called out, "Hey Jack… you there?"

It was Ryan.

"Over here," shouted Jack. "By the well."

Ryan came around the rockery. He was younger than Jack and not as tall, with frizzy blonde hair.

"I just tried phoning you. I heard this sort of crackling sound, and then got cut off."

Jack explained how he'd fallen, trying to retrieve his quadcopter.

"Well it looks like you managed to shake it loose," said Ryan, "it's down there by the wall."

Jack looked over, and saw the tiny craft propped up against the wall at the end of the bench, its lights still flashing. "Anyway, never mind that," said Jack, "I can't find my phone. It's really odd, I only had it in my hand a minute ago."

"Hang on, I'll call it," said Ryan, taking out his own phone and poking the screen. "OK, it should be ringing any minute now."

They listened intently for a while, but all they could hear was the familiar backdrop of sound made by the gentle boom of waves breaking down in nearby Halt Cove and the plaintive calls of the seagulls.

"This is crazy," said Jack, moving across to the other side of the patio and scratching his head. As he passed the well, he saw an orange glow at the bottom. He leant over the side and peered down into the gloomy interior.

"It's down here," he exclaimed.

"You're joking?" said Ryan, coming over to stand next to him.

"No. Look – see it? That orange glow."

"Oh yeah. That's the end of that then."

"I could climb down there," said Jack.

"There's no point, it's probably all busted up," said Ryan.

"It might not be, it's got that new case on. Anyway, it worked just now when you phoned it. We just need some rope."

Ryan gave in. He'd known Jack long enough to know that if he had set his mind on something, there was little point in trying to talk him out of it.

After fetching the workshop key from the drawer in the kitchen, they went off to search for a rope. They found a coil of it hanging on the back of the workshop door and took it back to the well. The well had two posts holding up a small tiled roof. It had once had a wooden bucket, which was lowered down into the well to collect water, but this had fallen to pieces and been removed.

Jack uncoiled the rope, passed it round one of the posts, and tied the end around his middle. He then handed the remaining coils of rope to Ryan and climbed onto the wall.

"You sure about this? It's a long way down," said Ryan, taking the rope from him.

"Yeah, I'll be fine," said Jack, swinging his legs over the well.

The post creaked as he slid off the wall. Ryan began to feed out the rope, slowly lowering him down into the well. It wasn't long before Jack could barely see the walls around him, and he wished he'd thought to bring a torch. A shiver ran through him. It was getting cooler, and the air was becoming musty and damp.

Ryan called down to him, his voice echoing. "Are you all right down there?"

"Yeah, it's getting a bit dark though," shouted Jack.

"I could go and see if I can find a torch."

"No, it's OK, just keep lowering. With any luck, I'll be able to use my phone as a torch on the way back up."

Several minutes later his feet touched the bottom, and became very wet. The water was ice cold. He shouted up to Ryan, "I'm at the bottom. Can you ring it again?"

Ryan's head appeared over the wall at the top. "OK. Hang on."

4

It was quiet in the well, with just the odd plop as water dripped into the shallow pool Jack was standing in. His phone suddenly sprang to life, lighting up the crystal-clear water. The bottom of the pool was mostly covered in small stones, but here and there he could see old bricks, some upended and poking up through the water. Jack wished he had more time to explore to see what else was down there, but his aunt and uncle would be back soon, and he didn't want them to catch him in the well.

He bent down and picked up his phone, and was pleased to see the screen was still in one piece. The toughened grey plastic cover he'd recently fitted had absorbed most of the impact, although it now had a small split in one corner. He flipped to the next screen, got the small torch light on it working, and then shone it around the well. He could see iron rungs sunk into the wall on the other side of the well, like a sort of ladder. He slid his phone into his shirt pocket with the light shining away from him, and called up to Ryan.

"I'm ready to come back up now. I can see rungs in the wall, so I'll use them to climb up."

"OK, I'll keep pulling in the slack," replied Ryan.

Jack started back up. Even with the rungs to hold on to and stand on, it was hard work. Some of the rungs had become loose in the brickwork, and a couple had rusted through, so he carefully tested each one before putting any weight on it. As he climbed higher, he could see that the rungs didn't go all the way to the top. He climbed up to the last rung, looped an arm through it, and shouted up to Ryan.

"There's no more rungs! I'll have to climb the rope for the last bit."

Ryan's head appeared over the wall. "OK, I'll tie it up around the post."

Jack took a breather. The bricks lining the well were very old and chipped at the edges, the cement around them falling out in places.

It was then that Jack noticed some unusual looking bricks further down. He climbed down a couple of rungs, pulled the phone from his top pocket, and shone the light from it directly onto them. They were golden-brown and had a peculiar glassy surface, which was covered in tiny dimples. They were smaller than the other bricks, and in an almost complete ring around the well. The cement holding them in place looked quite new.

One of the bricks a little further around appeared much darker. Jack moved the light over it and was amazed to see that it was just as dark with the light on it as it had been before. That was odd.

He twisted the phone around to check the light was still working, and was dazzled by the brightness of the beam. He tried bringing the light closer to the brick, but it made not the slightest difference – the brick still looked pitch black.

But then something happened. Green speckles started to appear inside the strange brick, and slowly drifted towards the centre, forming a ball. The ball shuddered; just the tiniest of movements, as if it was coming to life. It began to move around more vigorously, flying from side to side and from top to bottom, bouncing off the inside edges of the brick. It brightened, and then jumped to another brick. It jumped again, and then again, moving from one golden-brown brick to another around the well, going faster and faster, until there was a bright green ring surrounding him.

Jack shouted up to Ryan. "Ryan quick, come and look at this."

Ryan's head appeared over the wall at the top.

"What is it?"

"These bricks," said Jack excitedly. "Look - they're all lit up!"

"I can't see anything," said Ryan, sounding bored.

"You must be able to see it!"

"Nope. I can barely see you. Are you coming back up or what?"

The green ring began to fade, and for a moment Jack could have sworn he could see two dark eyes staring back at him from one of the bricks. Then the ring faded to black. Whoa, that was weird!

Jack hauled himself up the rope, and Ryan helped him out of the well.

"I saw something down there," said Jack.

"You mean those bricks?"

"Yes, they're not like the other bricks. They're sort of golden with a strange surface, and much smaller. And there was something inside them – I'm sure of it."

"Maybe you're seeing things. You did bang your head."

"No, there's definitely something down there."

At that moment, they heard a car coming up the drive. It was Uncle Fred and Aunt Lori returning from their shopping trip.

"We can't be found here," said Jack. "You fetch the quadcopter. I'll untie the rope."

They coiled up the rope, hid it under a conifer, and then ran down the garden. As they got to Jack's bedroom door Aunt Lori's voice sang out from the hall.

"Jack, we're back!"

The two boys sauntered down the stairs, acting as if they had been up there all the time. "Hello Ryan, I thought you were away on holiday," said Aunt Lori.

"I was – I mean we were. We just got back. The weather wasn't much good, it seemed to rain all the time."

"Where did you go?" asked Uncle Fred, putting a box of breakfast cereal into a kitchen cupboard to one side of the cooker.

"Camping with my dad. It rained every day we were there."

"Whereabouts?"

"In Wales, somewhere around Snowdon."

"Ah, it does seem to rain a lot around there, something to do with the mountain I believe."

While they were talking, Jack edged his way over to the drawer next to the back door, pulled it open and dropped the workshop key back inside. They had switched off the workshop light and locked the door again, so it would all look normal unless Uncle Fred spotted the rope was missing, which was pretty unlikely, since it had been covered by an old blanket, which Jack had hung back up again.

5

Jack came downstairs to find the house empty. He opened the back door and saw Uncle Fred kneeling at the side of the lean-to, patching up the hole that Cody had made. He had his wooden toolbox beside him. That was the one from the workshop, so it was probably unlocked, thought Jack. He saw his chance to return the rope. But as he stepped out of the back door, he was spotted by Uncle Fred.

"Ah, Jack, you're just in time. Here, hold on to this."

Jack walked over and took the thin plywood panel from him.

"If you could hold it over the hole," said Uncle Fred.

Jack knelt down and held the panel over the window frame with the broken glass.

"That's it. Over that way just a bit. That's right. Hold it just there."

Uncle Fred picked up a screw and began rummaging around in his toolbox. The tools were clanking against one another and knocking against the sides.

"I don't seem to have the right screwdriver here," he said. "Can you fetch it? It should be in the workshop. My large crosshead. You know – the one with the red handle."

Jack couldn't believe his luck. Placing the panel down on the ground, he set off down the garden. As he retrieved the rope from under the conifers, he spotted the cane he had been using lying on the ground close by. He carried the rope and the cane back to the workshop, throwing the cane on to the pile where he'd found it. After a quick search through the tools lying around the workshop, he found the screwdriver and took it back to his uncle.

"That's the one," said Uncle Fred, taking it from him. "Right, hold up the panel again."

Jack knelt down and offered up the panel. As he was watching his uncle screwing it on, his mind began to wander. He started thinking about the strange bricks he'd discovered in the well, and wondered if his uncle knew anything about them.

"Uncle."

"Yes?"

"You know the well."

"Yes," said Uncle Fred, a bit surprised by the question. "What of it?"

"When I was looking down it yesterday, I thought I saw some odd-looking bricks. They were sort of square and a light brown."

"They're a long way down," said Uncle Fred. "I'm surprised you can see them from the top."

"I shone a light down," said Jack, thinking how much trouble he would be in if his uncle knew how he'd really seen them. "I was just wondering if you knew anything about them?"

"It's a while back now. I noticed some of the bricks in the wall at the top of the well were loose, so I cemented them back in. I then got to thinking about what it might be like further down, so I hooked up a rig and went down there. It was a good thing I did, because it was in a pretty bad way. There were big gaps where the cement had fallen out, and some of the bricks were missing. While I was down in the village I bumped into Ruan Brock. He mentioned he was having trouble with one of his shearing machines, and asked if I would have a look at it. I drove over to Kettle Farm the next day and managed to fix it – the blades had jammed. I had time on my hands, so I thought I'd go up and visit the crater. We used to go there a lot when we were younger, your aunt and I – take picnics. Anyway, while I was up there, I saw one of those bricks sticking up out of the ground. There was only one, poking up through the mud, but when I dug around, I found more. I mentioned it to Ruan, and he said I could take whatever I liked. So, I brought a dozen or so back here and cemented them into the well. It was a big job, I can tell you."

At that moment someone called out, and Ryan came around the corner of the house. "Hi. I rang the front door bell, but there was no answer."

Jack turned to his uncle. "Is it all right to let go now?"

"Yes, I've got a couple of screws in, so it should stay up."

Jack got to his feet.

"Hang on," said Uncle Fred. "I've got something for you." He twisted around and picked up something off the ground. It was Cody's frisbee. "We found it in there," he said, handing it to Jack.

"Oh, thanks," said Jack, "I don't know how it got in there."

"Mmm," sighed Uncle Fred. "Well, just make sure it, doesn't find its way in there again."

When they were on their own, Jack told Ryan what his uncle had said about the bricks.

"So they're from the crater," said Ryan.

"Yeah. I think we ought to go up there, to see if there are any more. We can pick your bike up on the way."

Carey Lane was at the edge of Port Marron village and wound its way out towards the cliffs, while the main part of the village lay down in the bay. Jack's house was well over a hundred and fifty years old and sat towards the landward end, whereas Ryan's house was one of the more recent bay-fronted properties at the other end, nearer the sea. Despite living in the same lane, Jack and Ryan had never met until they bumped into one another at school. They hadn't got off to the best start, with Jack accidentally treading on Ryan's foot on his way into assembly. It had taken a little while, but Ryan had eventually forgiven him, and they had become the best of friends.

Ryan pressed the front doorbell and waited

for his mother to answer. He didn't have a key because he'd mislaid the last one, and his mother refused to give him another, which annoyed him no end.

There was no answer.

"She's probably down the studio," said Ryan.

The back gate was bolted at the top, but by standing on tiptoe Ryan was tall enough to reach over and unbolt it.

Mrs Gainer was a keen wood carver, and she had a large conservatory at the bottom of the garden, which she called her studio. She had begun carving as a hobby and soon discovered she had a real flair for it. She was sitting at a bench in the front window, working on an owl, carving out the intricate patterns on its wings with a fine chisel.

She looked up and smiled at them as they came through the door. "Hello Jack."

"Hi."

"Is everything OK, Ryan?"

"Yeah, I just need my bike. Have you got the key to the garage?"

"Yes, but be sure you lock it again, and bring the keys straight back here."

"Yes yes, all right," said Ryan.

Jack looked around the room as he waited for Ryan to return. A wooden tiger sat on its haunches at the end of a shelf near his shoulder, poised as if ready to attack, its front paws raised, showing its razor-sharp claws. Further along the shelf were more owls, some sitting like the one being carved and some flying. The biggest and most impressive carving was of an elephant. Too big to fit on a shelf, it stood on all fours near the door, as if to welcome visitors. It had been made from sheets of two different woods, one paler than the other, sandwiched together and glued, which gave it vertical stripes from the end of its trunk to the tip of its tail.

Jack spotted a line of eagles on a shelf near the window. They had been carved as if in flight, soaring, with their wings spread wide.

He picked one up.

"Are these for the Country Fair?"

"Yes, I'm flat out at the moment preparing for it,' said Mrs Gainer. 'What with that and organising the rest of the craft marquee, I've got my work cut out, I can tell you. Do you like it?"

"Yes, it's great."

"You can have it," she said.

"Are you sure?"

"Yes, I've got quite a lot of those."

"Thank you!" said Jack, a little taken aback.

"Is your aunt still OK for the fair?" asked Mrs Gainer.

"I think so," replied Jack.

"Good. Her bonsai trees are always very popular."

Ryan returned, holding the keys out and jingling them in front of him.

"Did you lock the garage again?" asked Mrs Gainer, taking them from him.

"Yes, of course I did," said Ryan, with an exaggerated smile, rocking his head from side to side.

"Where are you cycling to?" she asked, glaring at him.

"Just up to the crater," said Ryan.

"Well, mind how you go."

"OK, see you later then," said Ryan, making a quick exit.

"Bye," said Jack. "And thanks again for the eagle."

"You're welcome."

"Did my mum give you that?" asked Ryan, as they walked back up the garden.

"Yeah, it's amazing. She's really good."

6

Jack and Ryan made their way to the end of the road and then turned down Merry Lane. In a short while they could see Oak Field rising up steeply behind the hedgerow on the left-hand side. The gate was in the far corner, with the entrance to Kettle Farm, which owned the field, nearby. At the top of the field, looking as if it had been punched into the top by a giant fist, was the crater. It had been there so long that nobody really knew how it had been made. Some said it was where a bomb had been dropped during the war. Others said it had been made by a meteorite falling from outer space. However it had been made, being bowl-shaped, it made a great mountain bike track.

The path to the crater was too steep to cycle up, so they wheeled their bikes to the top. Jack was the first to arrive. He pulled a bottle of water from the clip on his bike and took a long swig.

"That path seems to get steeper every time we come up here," complained Ryan, staggering to a stop next to him.

Jack passed him the water bottle. They sat down on the grass with their backs to the crater, with Halt Cove sweeping around in front. Out to sea the waves frothed white as they broke against the seven jagged rocks known as the Seven Sisters Reef. The name was deceptive, because as well as the seven rocks you could see stretching out in a long line above the surface, there were more hidden just below, ready to hole the boat of any unwary mariner. Off to the right, the tip of the harbour wall down in Port Marron could be seen above the cliff, along with the roofs and chimneys of some of the houses.

A young seagull speckled with brown and white came down in the grass a short distance away and looked them over, obviously in the hope that they had something for it to eat. It stood watching them for several minutes as they drank from the water bottle, then, seeing they had nothing to offer, it flew away again.

A speedboat towing a skier came around the headland. The boat zig-zagged backwards and forwards across the bay, slicing and bouncing through its own bow waves, the skier behind skilfully jumping over them, bright flashes of sunlight reflecting off their skis.

"That looks fun," said Jack.

"Yeah. I reckon you've got to be a good swimmer before you can go out there and do that. You'd be all right."

Ryan knew that Jack was a good swimmer. Aunt Lori had insisted on him having swimming lessons when he had first come to live with them. Being able to swim hadn't seemed quite so important when he was living in London, but as she would say, 'living near the sea is different'.

When his aunt had first taken him to have lessons at the local swimming baths it had looked as if he would never learn, because he had found it impossible to stay afloat. Mr Whitley, his swimming instructor, hadn't helped by shouting instructions across the pool and telling him to push his bottom up, which had made him sink even more. But a few weeks after the lessons started, he was joined by another much younger swimming instructor called Joe. Joe had told Jack to just relax and trust the water to hold him up. He'd tried it, and found to his surprise that it helped him stay afloat. After that, with Joe's help, he'd found learning to swim a lot easier, and soon picked up the breast stroke, and then the crawl, although he still sometimes got a mouthful of water when he got the breathing wrong on the crawl.

The speedboat made one more pass across the bay, and then disappeared back around the headland. Jack got to his feet. "Shall I go first?"

"Yeah, go for it," said Ryan.

He picked up his bike, wheeled it over to a well-worn track at the rim of the crater, and then climbed on to the saddle. After checking his brakes, he launched himself over the edge. The bike surged forwards as he took off down the narrow mud track, snaking his way in and out of the small bushes growing up the side.

"Woohoo!" he shouted.

He levelled out as he reached the bottom, but the bike showed no signs of slowing. He weaved across the crater, carefully avoiding a large tree towards the middle, the long grass clinking musically against the spokes of his wheels. As he was approaching the other side of the crater, he swung the bike around sideways and skidded to stop.

"Phew. That was amazing!" he gasped.

Ryan appeared at the edge of crater and cycled down, following Jack's trail, and skidded to a stop next to him. "Whoa, I'd forgotten how good that was."

"Yeah, brilliant."

They started searching for the bricks. Most of the crater was covered in long grass, which made it very difficult to see the ground underneath. Jack thought he'd found one of them, but when he kicked it out of the ground, it turned out to be just an odd-shaped rock.

"Well, if they're here, they're well hidden," said Ryan, after they'd combed the bottom of the crater.

"Maybe they're up at the top," said Jack, now wishing he'd asked Uncle Fred where in the crater he had actually found the bricks.

They pushed their bikes back up the side of the crater, and then searched around the rim.

"I think he must have got them all," said Jack, after a while.

"Yeah, I was thinking the same thing," said Ryan.

They had several more rides down the sides of the crater, taking in some of the other tracks, and then headed back down the hill. Jack turned towards Ryan as they reached the gate at the bottom of the field. "I was thinking of going down to the harbour – the tide will be in about now."

"Yeah all right," said Ryan, "I'm in no rush to get back."

Cycling to the other end of Merry Lane, they turned down into Port Marron. The road to the harbour went around a slight bend and down steeply, becoming much narrower as it squeezed in between houses on each side. They passed a row of small slim houses facing the harbour, each distinguished from its neighbour by its own pastel colour of yellow, pink, green or orange, but they were all huddled together as if to keep out the cold that gripped them in the winter.

There was a small shop at the end of the row that sold ice creams. Jack pulled up in front of it and climbed off his bike. "I'm gonna have an ice lolly, do you want one?"

"If you're buying, I haven't got any money."

Jack bought himself a mango-flavoured ice lolly with ice cream down the middle, and Ryan chose a toffee ice cream cornet with a chocolate flake. They sat down to eat them on a low stone wall at the front of the shop, looking out over the harbour. The fishing boats were returning with their catch. Two boats had already moored up, and were busy unloading. Seagulls were wheeling and calling out above them, the more daring ones coming down to land near the crates of fish piling up on the quay, in the hope of stealing a tasty morsel.

Jack spotted the striped blue and white hull of the *Blue Angel* making its way into the harbour. Cadan was piloting it, a stocky man with an unruly reddish-brown beard who looked almost too big for the wheelhouse. They finished eating and cycled around to the quay to meet it.

As they were standing on the quayside watching the boats sail into the harbour there was a screech of brakes and Ethan Mathews skidded to a stop next to Jack, closely followed by Neil Willis. Jack wasn't pleased to see either of the two boys, who were a couple of years older than him. Ethan, tall with long dark hair, and a round face, which wore a permanent smirk, seemed to enjoy making his life a misery, and Neil would egg him on and laugh at his rubbish jokes.

"No nursemaid today then, Burrows?" said Ethan.

Jack knew he was talking about his aunt. He tried not to show he was bothered by the remark, but his face disobeyed him, and he flinched.

"Ooh, hit a nerve there Neil," said Ethan, looking very pleased with himself.

"Yeah," said Neil, grinning inanely, showing a large gap between his front teeth.

Pretending to be friendly, Ethan leant over and slapped Jack hard on the back, nearly knocking him off his saddle. "Not seen you around much this holiday. What you been up to then?"

"Oh, not much," said Jack, hoping that if he didn't say too much Ethan would lose interest and go away."

Ethan nodded towards the water behind Jack. "You here for a swim then?"

"No, just looking around," said Jack.

"Oh, I think you'd enjoy a swim," said Ethan. With that, he lashed out a foot, kicking Jack's rear wheel. The bike toppled over sideways and Jack came off, almost tripping over the handlebars as they came down in front of him. He struggled desperately to try to regain his balance, but he was too close to the edge of the quay, and fell with an enormous splash into the harbour.

Ethan and Neil snorted with delight. Ryan jumped off his bike and ran to the edge of the quay. Jack was treading water a little way out from the side, a look of shock on his face.

"You idiots!" shouted Ryan. He knelt down over the edge and shouted to Jack. "Here, grab my hand."

Although it was high tide the water was well below the quay, and Ryan had to lean over precariously to try to reach his friend. Ethan stepped up behind him and was about to use his knee to nudge him into the water to join his friend when someone hollered out from the harbour, and he changed his mind.

"Jack – over here!"

Jack turned in the water to see Cadan leaning over the side of the *Blue Angel*. He made a few strokes towards him. It was hard swimming fully clothed, and every sweep of his arms seemed to move him backwards as much as forwards, but he made it to the side of the boat and Cadan, grabbing hold of him with one hand, hoisted him out the water and plonked him down on deck.

With Jack safe, Cadan turned his attention to Ethan and Neil. "You fools!" he bellowed, his face turning bright red, competing strongly with his beard. "He could've drowned!"

Realising that it perhaps wasn't a good idea to stick around until the *Blue Angel* reached the quay, Ethan and Neil quickly mounted their bikes and took off, pedalling away frantically. The *Blue Angel* swung around, gently nudging up against the quayside. Cadan invited Ryan on board, and then made them both a hot drink.

"What's up with that kid?" asked Cadan, as they sat on crates drinking giant mugs of tea.

"I don't know, he's always like that," said Jack.

"He's not from round here."

"No, he lives on the other side of Kerstle," said Ryan. "At least that's where he gets on the school bus."

Jack was glad it was the summer holidays, as he hated travelling on the school bus, which was where Ethan seemed to be at his worst. Most of the seats were taken by the time Ethan got on, but no one dared refuse him if he asked them to move. That meant that no matter where Jack and Ryan sat they'd find Ethan, along with his sidekick Neil, sitting either in front or behind them, making their trip to school a misery.

Cadan left them and went to organise the off-loading of today's catch. It was a while since Jack had been on board the *Blue Angel*. When his uncle had been the skipper, he'd often sailed with him, and he had fond memories of his time on board. Looking around he could see the wheelhouse had been repainted, but apart from that, as far as he could see, everything looked the same.

The crew were hauling large green plastic crates over the side and stacking them up on the quay, each one brimming with lobsters. Each lobster had yellow rubber bands around its claws to hold them shut. Lobsters that were spoiled wouldn't fetch as much, so the bands were put on to stop them fighting. It had been one of the jobs that Jack had learnt to do, placing the bands over the claws with a special pair of pliers so he didn't lose a finger.

They walked over and leant against the boat rail to watch the catch being offloaded.

Cadan was talking to the owner of a small van that had pulled up on the quay, negotiating a price. Jack and Ryan climbed over the side of the boat and jumped down to the quay.

"We'll be off then," said Jack, "thanks again for rescuing me."

"You're welcome. You stay clear of that one from now on – oh, and say hello to your uncle for me."

"I will," said Jack.

Jack checked inside his jacket to make sure his carved eagle was okay. It was very wet, but still in one piece. He was soaked to the skin, and as they pedalled home, he could feel water sloshing about inside his trainers.

When he got home, he managed to sneak in through the back door and up to his room to change into dry clothes without being noticed. Aunt Lori gave him a funny look when he appeared in the kitchen wearing a different pair of jeans and T-shirt. He thought for a moment that she was going to say something, but a saucepan came to his rescue, boiling over on the hob. By the time she'd rushed over to it to turn down the heat, she'd forgotten all about it. He'd put his wet clothes and trainers on the radiator under his window, in the hope that they would be dry by the morning, and sat the eagle on the window-sill.

7

Jack was woken from a restless sleep. Something was wrong, very wrong. He was awake, but he felt as if he was still in the middle of some crazy dream. He had no control over what he was doing. It was as if his body was doing someone else's bidding, and he was just a puppet. It sat up, swung its legs over the edge of the bed and stood up. His feet walked him across the bedroom floor to the door, where his arm reached out and opened it. He was then taken downstairs. Still dressed only in his pyjamas, he padded barefoot across the kitchen floor, unlocked the back door, and stepped out into the cool night air. He didn't feel the cold, he didn't really feel anything at all; he seemed to be numb to almost everything.

His body walked him down the garden. He watched each foot as it planted itself down on the ground, and then disappeared below him as he stepped forwards. He should be the one doing that – what was going on?

At the rear of the rockery, his feet stopped. At that moment he felt that his body had been returned to him, but still he couldn't move, because he was transfixed by the weird sight in front of him. The concrete slabs in front of the well were glowing bright green, and there was something moving about inside them.

Then a worm-like creature seemed to wriggle up through the ground. Its body was translucent and there was a shimmering green light at one end. The furthest end swung around to reveal a flat face with two small black eyes, like the ones he had seen in the well.

"Do not be alarmed," it said. The words did not seem to be transmitted by sound; it was more as if the strange high-pitched voice was appearing inside Jack's head.

The creature spoke slowly and calmly.

'I have brought you here to ask for your help,' it said. 'Our spaceship has crash-landed here on your planet. We were carrying a creature, and after we crashed, it managed to free itself, trapping us inside these rocks, so it could make its escape. This creature is extremely dangerous and must be recaptured. But I cannot do this alone, I will need help from the others, who are still trapped down there. Since you freed me, I have felt a great energy above this place. If you could capture this energy and bring it to them, I should be able to do the rest. Please, you must help us!'

The worm slid back below the slabs, and disappeared. Jack stood staring at the spot it had occupied, his head spinning from the strange encounter. He stumbled back down the garden and back to his room.

Once safely back in his bed, he lay pondering on what the worm had told him. What did it mean by 'great energy above this place'? There was nothing above the well, only sky. Sky, clouds, and the... He suddenly realised what the worm had meant by the great energy – it must be the Sun. So, the light from his phone had freed it, and it needed more light to free the others. But how? Maybe, he could capture the light from the Sun with mirrors, and beam it down the well. He would ask his uncle about mirrors in the morning.

Despite the strange encounter, now that he had things sorted out in his head, he quickly went off to sleep.

***

Uncle Fred looked up from drilling a piece of metal clamped in the vice. "What do you want with mirrors?"

"I thought I'd use them to reflect light down the well," said Jack, "to see if I can see any more of those bricks."

"Well, I can't see any harm in that," said Uncle Fred, pleased that his nephew shared his inquisitive nature. "Now, where have I seen mirrors recently?" he went on, looking up at the ceiling as if the answer might be written on it. "Ah, yes, I know, the solar-powered cooker. The mirrors are curved, so you'll probably need to flatten them out. I think I saw it over there last." He nodded towards the rear of the workshop.

Jack found what was left of the old solar cooker leaning against the back wall, and went to work on it. The pot for the food and the bracket used to hold it were missing, but the two curved metal mirrors, one on each side, were still in place. He unbolted them and stood on each one to flatten it, then carried them out to the well. He took some string and made two loops, tying them around the horizontal beam between the posts holding up the roof. Picking up one of the mirrors, he slid it into the loops, so it faced it down into the well. He then put the other mirror down on the ground at the side. The sky was still cloudy, but the sun was beginning to push through.

Ryan arrived.

"What you doing?"

Jack wasn't sure if he should tell Ryan his plan. He had got the impression that Ryan didn't believe there was anything strange down the well, and thought his friend was seeing things.

"I want to see if I can see any more of those bricks, so I thought I'd rig up some mirrors to reflect the light down there."

"Oh. Are you sure it'll work?"

"I think it will. I just need to get them at the right angle."

Uncle Fred appeared around the rockery. "I just came to see if you needed a hand, but it looks like you've got it covered."

"We're just waiting for the sun to come out," said Jack.

"Oh, right. Well give me a call if you need anything. I'll be in the workshop."

The sun peeped out from behind a cloud, but there were more clouds rolling up and Jack wasn't sure how long it would be before it went in again. He bent down and lifted up the far side of the mirror, then tilted it towards the well, sending a dazzling flash of sunlight across Ryan's face.

"Whoa, careful!" said Ryan.

"Sorry," said Jack. "Can you see if you can find some rocks to prop it up? I think there's some towards the back of the rockery over there."

Ryan returned moments later with a couple of rocks. "Will these do?"

"Yeah, perfect."

Jack put the rocks under the mirror, one at each end, so that it was fixed at the correct angle to reflect sunlight on to the mirror hanging above the well.

"Wow," said Ryan, looking down into the well. "I didn't expect it to be that bright. You can almost see all the way to the bottom."

The sun disappeared behind a cloud, and the well went dark again.

"Oh, that's a shame," said Ryan, "I didn't get a chance to see those bricks."

"It might clear up later on," said Jack. "We'll leave the mirrors there, then if it comes out again, we can have another go."

Cody came to his side and stood with his front paws up on top of the wall.

"What shall we do while we're waiting?" asked Ryan.

Jack nodded at Cody. "How about taking him down the beach?"

8

The closest beach was Halt Cove, which was just beyond Oak Field. As they walked along the narrow winding path down to the beach, Cody could smell the sea and kept pulling on his lead. Jack unclipped it at the bottom of the path and Cody ran around in circles barking excitedly before dashing down the beach to greet the waves.

Catching up with him, Jack picked up a flat grey pebble and sent it skimming across the water. Cody ran after it, lolloping through the waves. It bounced once, twice, three times and then sank, and he stood looking confused at the spot where it had vanished. Ryan picked up a lump of driftwood and threw it out to him, and Cody chased it down, bringing it back to dry land proudly between his teeth. Ryan threw the lump of wood out again. Cody ran backwards and forwards into the waves countless times retrieving it and attempting to bury it before finally giving up and sinking down onto the sand.

"I think he's had enough," said Jack.

A tall, rocky promontory divided the cove in two. It was craggy with some great rock pools along the sides, so they made their way over to it to see what the tide had left behind. Cody noticed a seagull dozing on top. With several bounds he leapt up the side and ran towards it, barking. The gull, woken by the unexpected disturbance, took to the air, squawking noisily in protest.

As usual Cody was keen to poke his nose into every rock pool the boys showed any interest in. They took turns holding him back while the other explored the pools so that he didn't frighten away the sea life. They found a handful of shrimps, a small green crab that managed to nip Jack's finger as he picked it up, and a little fish, which Ryan thought might be a blenny. Cody started to whimper, so Jack let him loose to explore for a while, then they climbed back down to the beach.

They found a dry patch of sand further up, nearer the cliff, and sat down. Cody dug holes in the sand, and then came and slumped down next to Jack, panting. It was peaceful, with just the gentle crash of the waves as they swept in over the shingly threshold of the beach. Jack dreamily tracked a long ship as it sailed along the horizon, looking as if it was negotiating a tightrope between the sea and the sky.

He turned around to find Cody missing. "You seen Cody?" he said to Ryan.

"No, he was there a minute ago."

Jack called out to him. "Cody, here boy!"

But Cody didn't come to the call. Thinking

he might be too far away to hear him, Jack put two fingers in his mouth and blew, producing a shrill whistle. Cody still didn't come, so they set off down the beach to look for him. They found him further along the beach, up inside a small alcove under the cliff. Jack saw a piece of chicken protruding from the corner of his mouth.

"Drop it!" shouted Jack.

Cody swallowed it.

Jack ran over and grabbed his collar, and then looked around to see where he might have scavenged the chicken from. There was a small pile of blackened wood further up the alcove, under the cliff. He walked over to it, pulling Cody along at the side of him.

"Someone's had a barbecue," said Jack. It was then that he noticed a narrow gap in the cliff. He turned to Ryan. "Can you take him a minute?"

"Why, what is it?"

"There's a crack in the cliff. I think it might be a cave."

The crack ran up vertically and was wedge shaped, narrower at the bottom than at the top. He put his head inside it. He could see light.

"There's light in there," said Jack, his voice echoing. "I'm going in."

The gap was much narrower than he had thought, and he had to shuffle through sideways. The walls and ceiling were formed from pink and grey slate. After a few feet it began to widen out, but then Jack found his way blocked by an enormous boulder. The light seemed to be coming from behind it. Using a foothold in the wall, he hoisted himself up on top. He was about to jump down at the other side when he heard scratching, and Cody's head popped out below.

"You found your way in then," said Jack.

Ryan called from the other side of the boulder. "Have you got Cody in there?"

"Yeah, he just popped his head out underneath here."

Ryan scrambled up to join his friend. "Looks

like the light's coming from somewhere near the back," he said.

They jumped down. The narrow cave they were in opened out into a larger cave with a domed roof. A pile of pink slate was resting against the back wall where part of the roof had fallen in. There was a narrow shaft rising like a chimney where it had fallen away, and daylight was filtering down through it. They stood underneath peering upwards in the hope of seeing the sky, but a section of the shaft projected inwards, blocking the view.

"There must be a hole up in the cliff top," said Ryan.

"Yeah," said Jack eagerly. "Let's see if we can find it."

They retraced their steps out of the cave, then followed the path up to the cliff top and started to explore further around the bay in search of the hole.

"I reckon it should be about here," said Jack, stopping next to a wooden bench at the side of the path.

Jack tied Cody to the bench so he couldn't follow them, and they started searching for the hole. Suddenly Ryan let out a cry and disappeared.

"Jack!" he shouted, "I think I've found it!"

Jack rushed over to see that Ryan had fallen into a crescent-shaped hollow in the cliff top where the ground had subsided. He was lying on his back with his legs in the air, wedged in by the grass bank at each side. Jack couldn't help laughing to see his friend on his back, waving his arms and legs in the air like a stranded beetle.

"Yeah, very funny I'm sure," said Ryan. "If you can stop laughing long enough, maybe you can give me a hand up out of here."

"Sorry," said Jack. "it's just you look so funny."

He helped him out.

"Thanks," said Ryan, gruffly.

At the other end of the hollow was a dark opening. They walked over to it, and peered down it.

"It was lucky you didn't fall here," said Jack, "I reckon you could've gone down that."

"Yeah," said Ryan. "Do you think it's the hole down to the cave?"

"I think it must be," said Jack. Looking inland, he saw the clouds were dispersing, leaving patches of blue sky. "We ought to be getting back to the well, the sun's starting to push through."

***

When they got back to the well, the sun was no longer shining on the mirror and the well shaft was dark.

"The mirror needs adjusting," said Jack. "The sun's moved round."

They repositioned the mirror, and the golden-brown bricks sparkled again as the sunlight caught it.

"I see what you mean about those bricks," said Ryan, peering down into the well. "They are a bit weird."

"So, do you believe I saw something now?"

"I don't know. You've got to admit, it was a bit odd."

Jack decided to tell Ryan what had happened in the night. Ryan listened in silence, his jaw dropping in astonishment.

"And this worm thing *talked* to you?" he said, unable to take it in.

"Well, it didn't actually talk. It's hard to describe. I could hear its voice – you know, in my head."

The tiny sparkles from the sunlight on the bricks were once again making a bright ring around the inside of the well. They watched it for a while, hoping they would see Jack's worm, but there was no sign. The mirror on the ground needed to be adjusted every few minutes to track the sun. Eventually they got bored with all this and to occupy Cody, they played a game of 'piggy in the middle' on the lawn, with Cody playing the piggy. He was good at it, jumping high and snatching the ball out of the air with his teeth. He didn't always let them have the ball back, but trying to wrestle it off him while he faked a growl was all part of the game.

Soon the sun was beginning to fade. The sky had remained almost cloudless all afternoon, and by repeatedly adjusting the mirror they had successfully beamed several hours of sunlight down the well on to the strange bricks.

"Well, if that doesn't work, I don't know what will," said Jack, pulling the mirror from its loops at the top of the well.

"How do we know if it's worked?" asked Ryan.

"I don't know," said Jack, "maybe I'll see something tonight."

They carried the mirrors back to the workshop.

***

Late that night Jack was watching from his bedroom window, sitting on the windowsill with his feet up and his back against the wall. There didn't appear to be anything happening down at the well.

He was about to give up and crawl back into bed when a green glow appeared under the conifers. A worm!

Jack watched as the strange creature slid steadily up inside the trunk of one of the conifers, just as if it was inside an invisible lift. It stopped near the top, as if looking out for something, and then came back down. Another worm appeared beside it, and then another and another, until there was a big green squirming ball of them at the bottom. Then one of the worms broke free and moved off towards the bottom of the garden, and the rest peeled off and followed. Soon they were stretching out like a long string of luminous green beads across the field beyond it. Jack realised that they were heading towards the crater. Within a few minutes they had reached the hill in Oak Field.

Jack watched as they climbed it and

disappeared one by one inside the crater. He sat watching a little longer, but couldn't see any more signs of them. Finally he went back to bed, his mind buzzing with the mystery of what he had just witnessed.

***

He was woken by a loud clap of thunder. Rain was hammering against the window in the darkness, and the room was alive with lightning. It was cosy in bed, and he didn't want to get out, but the top window was open, and he wasn't going to get any sleep if he didn't close it.

Reluctantly he got out of bed and walked across to the window. As he was reaching up to close it, there was an enormous flash of lightning which lit up the garden and the surrounding countryside as if it were the middle of the day. In that fleeting moment he saw what looked like a giant tripod in the distance above the crater. Each one of its enormous legs had a string of green spots down it – were they the worms?

The outlandish structure seemed to be attracting the storm towards it, and black clouds were gathering and swirling around it. As he watched, a bolt of lightning flashed down and struck the top, turning several of the green spots bright orange. More direct hits followed, each one making more of the spots change colour. Then, as if destroyed by the intense bombardment, the whole thing slowly sank down into the crater. The lightning stopped, but the rain continued.

9

Jack rose early, eager to investigate the scene outside and wondering what he might find at the crater. He got dressed, and then called Cody out of his bed. As he got to the bottom of the stairs, he could hear Aunt Lori humming to herself in the sitting room.

"I'm just taking Cody out for a walk," he shouted.

"OK, be careful. There was a lot of rain in the night, so it might be a bit slippy."

Jack was dying to tell Ryan what he had seen in the night. Arriving at Ryan's house, he rang the front door bell. Mrs Gainer opened the door.

"Hello Jack."

"Hi, is Ryan around?"

"I don't think he's up yet. You're welcome to come in and wait for him."

"Oh, no I won't come in, I've got Cody. Can you tell him I'm going up to the crater?"

"Yes of course."

Ryan called down from upstairs. "Is that Jack?"

"Yes. He says he's going up to the crater."

"I'll meet you up there," hollered Ryan.

"I expect you heard that," said Mrs Gainer.

"Yeah," said Jack, smiling. He thanked Mrs Gainer, and then carried on to the crater.

When he arrived at Oak Field he was surprised to see a police van parked up on the grass in front of the gate. A police officer, Mr Brock and a girl with long bright ginger hair were standing at the bottom of the field. There was a flock of sheep nearby, and three of them were lying motionless on the ground.

The girl looked over at him as he came through the gate, and then returned her gaze to the sheep, which were not moving. Jack continued on up to the crater.

There were three distinct burnt patches around the rim of the crater. Each patch was circular and had wavy lines radiating out around the edges, making it look like a child's drawing of the sun. He wondered if the patches were in the places where the feet of the tripod had stood. He walked around to the nearest one to inspect it. The grass had been badly scorched, and came away easily in his hand.

He heard a shout behind him, and turned to see the police officer walking towards him. He was looking a little unsteady on his feet, and swaying.

"I'd, er, like... a word, young man," he said, gasping for breath. He was a short, plump man with rosy cheeks. He took off his hat showing a bald head, and wiped away the sweat from his forehead with his cuff.

"Yeah, sure," said Jack.

"Looks like the lightning struck here last night," said the policeman, looking at the burnt patch on the ground.

"Yes," said Jack. He was hoping that the officer wouldn't spot the other burnt patches and see how evenly spaced they were.

The officer replaced his hat and took a small notebook from his top pocket. "It's Jack, isn't it?"

"Eh... yes. That's right," said Jack, amazed that he knew his name.

"I pulled you over a while back," he said. "If I remember right, you were riding your bike with another boy on the back." He bent down and patted Cody. "This your dog?" he asked.

"Yes," said Jack.

"Do you keep him in at night?"

"Yes, he sleeps in my room," said Jack.

"Good, good. I don't suppose you've seen any other dogs around here lately - maybe going near the sheep?"

"No, I don't think so."

"You see, a number of sheep have died up here recently," he continued, "and it looks like something might have scared them to death. There's no marks on them, see." He stood there with his pencil hovering above his notebook, obviously hoping Jack would give him some information that would help him to solve the case.

"Maybe it was the lightning," said Jack, "they say some animals can die of fright."

"Hmm, it's possible I suppose. Well, keep a look out, and if you see anything let me know. You can contact me at Poldreath Police Station – Constable Harkin."

"Oh, right," said Jack. "Yes, I will."

PC Harkin smiled, sliding the notebook back into his pocket. "Don't forget now – you see anything suspicious, let me know." With that he turned and walked away, retracing his steps until he had disappeared over the edge of the crater.

Jack walked around the rim of the crater to another of the burnt patches. As he was inspecting it, Ryan appeared over on the other side of the crater. He dropped his bike on the ground and came over. "I've just been questioned by the police," he said. "Something about sheep dying."

"Yeah, he asked me as well," said Jack. "I couldn't really help him."

"No, me neither," said Ryan. "That was some storm last night. Is this where the lightning struck?"

"Sort of," said Jack. He told Ryan what he'd seen in the night.

"So, these burnt patches are where the legs of the tripod were standing?"

"I think they might be."

"So where are the worms now?" asked Ryan.

"They're probably searching for that creature," said Jack.

Cody started growling. He was looking at something on the other side of the crater, and he had his hackles up. Jack looked across to see what was bothering him. There was a bright patch of red light moving down the side.

"What's up with him?" asked Ryan.

"There's something over there."

The patch of light reached the bottom and started moving across the crater towards them. As it got closer, Jack saw that it wasn't a single patch of light as he'd first thought, but a cluster of bright red spots. They appeared to be moving along, but not on the ground – it looked as if they were under it.

"It's down there," said Jack, keeping his voice low, as the red spots were now directly below them.

There's nothing there," said Ryan. "Look, I'll show you." Before Jack could stop him, he picked up a rock and threw it down into the crater. The rock sailed through the air and landed with a thud. As it struck the bottom there was an ear-splitting screech, and a long, faceless creature appeared. It had a flat translucent body that was covered in bright red bumps.

"Whoa, what's that?" cried Ryan.

"RUN!" shouted Jack, taking off down the

hill, Cody running at his side. The sheep scattered, bleating noisily as they ran towards them.

"Over there," shouted Jack, "the tree in the corner."

The tree was an old oak at the corner of the field, which they had climbed many times before. The branches were thick, and the lower ones were in easy reach. Jack climbed up into it and patted a branch, and without any more encouragement Cody leapt up on to it, Ryan following swiftly behind him. They climbed further up the tree.

"That must be the creature the worm warned me about," said Jack, as they perched on a branch about halfway up, looking down through the leaves.

"Yeah. Can you still see it? What's it doing now?"

"It seems to be circling the tree," said Jack.

The creature was moving effortlessly through the ground just under the surface, leaving a fuzzy, translucent trail in its wake.

The ground was taking several seconds to turn solid again. Cody was sitting between them, lodged in a fork in the branch. He was watching the creature closely, following its every move.

"It looks like Cody can see it as well," said Jack.

The tree suddenly shook violently. Jack grabbed the branch in front of him and held on to Cody's collar with his other hand, to steady him.

The creature had surfaced and thrown itself against the tree. The tree shuddered a second time as the creature slammed into it again. It sat almost motionless for a while, and then, as if regaining its strength, it reared up and crashed against the trunk again. It struck the tree several more times, and then everything went quiet.

Jack peered down through the leaves. "I can't see it any more."

"Maybe it's gone," said Ryan, hopefully.

"Yeah," said Jack. "Let's hope so. I think

we ought to stay up here a bit longer, just to make sure."

They sat quietly, with Jack keeping look out for any movement below.

Ryan swore, breaking the silence. "Damn, I left my bike up there."

"You're joking!"

"No. I forgot all about it in the panic to get away from that thing."

"Well, we can't just leave it there, we'll have to go back up there and get it."

Keeping an eye out for the creature in case it returned, they climbed down the tree, and warily made their way back to the crater.

10

Cody made a deep rumbling growl as they approached the crater. Ryan patted him on the head. "It's all right Cody, it's gone now."

There was a bright flash as something caught the sun at the side of the crater. Jack cupped a hand against his forehead, and squinted. The bit of ground where he'd seen the flash was shimmering, like a mirage.

"What is it?" asked Ryan.

"I saw something over there."

"It's not that creature again?" said Ryan, looking worried.

"No, I saw a flash."

He made a mental note of its position, and then walked further round the crater.

"I think it was down there," he said, peering over the edge next to a small bush. He clipped on Cody's lead and handed it to Ryan.

"It looks slippery," said Ryan, taking the lead from him. "Are you sure you want to go down there?"

"Yeah, I've got to know what it is," said Jack.

The ground was treacherous, as it was still wet from the intense downpour in the night. After dropping down over the edge he was reluctant to let go of the small straggly bush he was holding on to, but he wanted to know what he'd seen. He grabbed a handful of wet grass with his other hand, let go, and started to make his way warily down the side.

He hadn't gone very far when his feet lost their grip. He slid down the side, grasping wildly at anything that might stop him. Halfway down, his feet bumped into something that arrested his fall. He pushed himself up on to his elbows and looked up. Ryan was now some distance away.

"You OK?" shouted Ryan.

"Yeah, just a bit muddy."

He looked down to see what had broken his fall, expecting to see a tree stump, a rock, or something sticking up out of the ground, but there was nothing there. That was odd. The side of the crater had levelled out slightly, making it a little easier to stand. He got to his feet, and felt around. His hands touched something hard. To Ryan watching from above, it looked like he was miming something.

"What are you doing?" Ryan asked incredulously, wondering if his friend had gone mad.

"There's something here."

"I can't see anything?"

"Neither can I. It's invisible."

"Hang on, I'm coming down."

Jack thought the strange invisible object

felt taller in the middle, while the top edge seemed to curve down to the ground at each side. It also seemed to be thinner front to back. Cody, having trotted down in a beeline from the top, joined him, having made the climb down look ridiculously easy. He wagged his tail enthusiastically, obviously thinking the whole thing was some kind of game. He bounced up and licked Jack's cheek, almost knocking him over.

"Yes, good boy... that's it. Sit... now stay."

Ryan climbed down cautiously, following a similar path to Jack's, but managing to stay on his feet.

"Right, where's this thing you've found?"

Jack took hold of Ryan's wrist and moved his hand to the top edge. "There – feel it?"

"Whoa! That's weird. It feels smooth."

"I think it might be part of the worm's spaceship," said Jack. "It seems to be stuck in ground, but I reckon we might be able to lift it out. If you lift here, I'll make my way to the other side and lift from there."

"Are you sure this is a good idea?" asked Ryan. "It's not going to be easy lifting something we can't see."

"Yeah, it'll be fine," said Jack.

Jack shuffled across, placing his feet against the invisible object for support. Cody was standing a short distance away, looking intrigued.

"OK," said Jack. "Ready. After three. One, two, three..."

The object moved upwards slightly, then Ryan's hands slipped off and it fell back down into the ground.

"It's really heavy," said Ryan.

"Yeah. But we nearly had it then."

Ryan moved his hands further down to get a better grip, and then they tried again.

"It's moving," grunted Jack.

Suddenly they felt the invisible thing shoot up out of the ground. It twisted around, slipping out from their hands and they heard it bump off down the side of the crater. It was rolling and quickly gathered speed, leaving a narrow track in the mud behind it. Cody ran after it, weaving backwards and forwards and barking excitedly. When the thing reached the bottom, it rolled onwards across the crater, revealing its path as it pushed the grass aside. For a minute it looked as if it was going to hit the tree in the middle, but then it seemed to hit a bump and veered off towards a large hawthorn bush. The bush shook violently, and then, as if by magic, a circular patch of flattened grass appeared to one side.

"Come on," shouted Jack, "let's go and see what we've got."

As they got nearer, they could hear a faint humming. Ryan stopped a short distance away. "I don't think we should go any nearer," he said warily.

Cody was crouching at side of the patch of flattened grass. Jack called to him. "Cody! Here boy."

Cody looked around, and then looked back at the patch. He was happy to stay put.

As they looked on, the humming stopped,

and a large silver disc materialised. A small hatch near the outer rim was open, and the boys could see an orange glow inside it. A ramp came into view and was lowered to the ground, and then a small, black furry head appeared. It had pointed ears that curved downwards, and a black shiny bulbous snout with white whiskers. It turned and looked up at them with sharp emerald-green eyes.

Jack heard words forming inside his head.

Are you the beings responsible for my release?

The creature was somehow communicating with him.

"Eh... Yes... I mean... we are," he stammered, taken aback by the strange deep voice and the way it had come to him without him hearing any sound.

Well. I thank you. But I could have done without being spun around quite so much.

More of the strange creature came into view as it proceeded slowly down the ramp. It was covered with black fur, streaked with grey, and about the size of a squirrel. The fur down the middle of its back and its broad tail was longer and thicker, and tipped with orange. It was wearing a gold band around the top of one arm. It stepped off the ramp, stood up on its back legs, and then unfurled two leathery wings, stretching them out and giving out a lengthy sigh.

Ahhh! I have been waiting a long time to do that. The creature stood for a while with its wings out, and then folded them back in again. *My name is Arkus,* it stated grandly.

They shuffled forwards.

"My name's Jack, and this is Ryan," said Jack.

"Is... is this a spaceship?" asked Ryan.

Yes. A Venya Class 1 Prison Ship. We were passing through your galaxy when we encountered an unusually large asteroid belt. Falon set a course to take us through them, but it was too dense. We struck one of the asteroids and were knocked off course, and crash-landed here. The impact knocked out most of

Falon's system, including communications, so we were left stranded.

"Who's Falon?" asked Jack.

Ah, yes, sorry, replied Arkus. *Falon is the on-board computer.*

He proceeded to walk around the spaceship, bending down to peer underneath it.

Ah, just as I thought, most of the cells on this side of the ship have been discharged. No matter, they are probably scattered somewhere around this crater. The prisoners should still be secured safely inside them.

Jack got down on his front and peered underneath the strange craft. The bottom of the spaceship was golden-brown, and it had a large bulge in the middle, leaving a gap between the outer rim and the ground. There was a ring of square holes around the outer rim. Jack noticed that the holes towards the other side of the ship had something inside them. The things inside the holes were the same colour as the bottom, which made them look like they were almost part of the ship.

He looked towards the tiny creature, which was standing a short distance away peering at him with interest. "So, the cells fit in under here?"

Yes, that is correct. They slide into those bays.

"The prisoners have to be quite small to fit into those cells," said Jack.

Ah, yes, I can see why you might think that. But in my world, we have developed technology that allows us to overcome the need to transport things at their normal size. It is called a Garner Ray. This ray breaks down and reorganises the makeup of things, shrinking them. The prisoners are first placed into a state of equilibrium, a trance-like state. They are then shrunk, and beamed into a cell. If something should go wrong on board, and the ship is in danger, the cells are automatically jettisoned. Each cell is fully autonomous, so it will continue to provide life support, and maintain the size of the occupant.

Jack now realised that the bricks his uncle had found and used to repair the well were not bricks at all, but were the jettisoned cells from Arkus' spaceship. He got back to his feet, and then thought he should to tell Arkus about one of the creatures escaping.

"One of your prisoners has escaped," he said.

What! cried Arkus.

"One of your crew told me – they said it was dangerous."

Crew! exclaimed Arkus. *I have no crew! Falon controls all functions on board the ship – under my command of course. I think you had better tell me what has been going on here.*

Jack told Arkus how he'd seen the strange bricks in the well, and how he had released the worms from them and then seen the unusual pointed structure above the crater. He also told him about the creature in the crater that had chased them.

Arkus nodded. *Ah. I'm afraid you have been deceived. The worm-like creatures, we call them Ky, that you set free, were the prisoners we were transporting.*

"But... but what about the other creature," stammered Jack, "the one that chased us?"

The Ky and the creature you saw are one and the same. Perhaps I had better explain. The Ky have the power to transform into another creature. The pointed edifice you saw above the crater, I believe you called it a tripod, is created by Ky linking, coming together, one Ky to another. They use this shape to create a storm, and then use its energy to change into this other creature, which we call a Torg. This Torg is extremely dangerous, it feeds on the life force of other living beings.

Jack and Ryan looked horrified. "Do you mean that thing could have killed us?" cried Ryan.

No, not at present, it is too young. But given time, it will become powerful enough to kill you, and your kind. It will also produce another Torg, an exact copy of itself, a clone.

"How long have we got before that happens?" asked Jack.

Several months.

"But where do they come from?" asked Ryan.

The Ky? We do not know their exact origin. Some time ago, we launched a probe into space, to investigate a nearby galaxy. Unfortunately, the probe malfunctioned. It veered off course, and we lost track of it. It eventually returned to our planet carrying the Ky. At first it looked like we were going to lose the battle against them. The Torg, the creature they become, moved around underground where we could not reach them, picking us off one by one. The future looked bleak for our kind. But then we came up with the idea of using the Garner Ray as a weapon. It was the breakthrough we had been hoping for, allowing us to both detect and destroy Torg underground. It was a long and bloody battle, but we eventually defeated them. We rounded up the remaining Ky for transportation to another planet, a planet where they could cause no harm.

"And you were on your way to this planet when you struck the asteroid?" said Jack.

Yes. Now, I must track down this creature.

He touched the gold band around the top of his arm, and the ramp slid back up inside the spaceship, the hatch closing behind it. He touched another part of the band and the spaceship became invisible again.

After moving a short distance away, he unfolded his wings. *I shall let you know if I need any help.* And with that, he took to the air.

The boys watched him spiral upwards, slowly becoming a speck in the sky. Then they climbed up the side of the crater, picked up Ryan's bike, and walked back down the hill.

As they came out through the gate and joined Merry Lane, someone called out to them.

"What were you doing up there?"

They turned to see the girl with ginger hair

leaning over the farm gate.

"What?" asked Jack, a little surprised by her rather blunt manner.

"I've seen you around here a lot recently," she said. "You were running across the field earlier. It looked like you were running away from something."

"We weren't running from anything," said Jack defensively. "Anyway, what's it got to do with you?"

"This is my dad's field."

"Ah, you're Ruan Brock's daughter," said Jack.

"Yes. My name's Kerra."

"I'm Jack, and this is Ryan," said Jack, thinking they'd somehow got off on the wrong foot, and that giving their names would get them on to the right one.

"So why were you running?" demanded Kerra, proving him wrong. "I have to ask, because we found some dead sheep up there this morning, and we're trying to find out what happened to them."

For a moment Jack considered telling her about the Torg, but then he thought better of it. "We were racing to see who could get down the hill first."

"Who won?" Kerra asked.

"Er... I did," said Jack.

"Mmm," said Kerra, frowning.

"Anyway, we'd better be getting back," said Jack, before she could ask any more questions. "See you around."

"She was a bit off," said Ryan, as they made their way down the lane.

"Yeah, she was, wasn't she?"

As they pulled up outside Ryan's house, Ryan turned to Jack. "I almost forgot. My dad's taking me sea fishing tomorrow, so I won't be around."

"Oh, okay. Well don't fall in."

Coming in through the back door, Jack found his aunt and uncle sitting at the kitchen table. Aunt Lori looked up.

"Ah, there you are. We've had sausages for lunch - is that OK for you?"

"Yeah, sound's great."

Cody trotted over to the table and sat looking up at Uncle Fred expectantly as he mopped sausage grease up from around his plate with his last piece of bread, then popped it into his mouth. Jack sat down at the other side of the table. Realising that Uncle Fred had finished, Cody shifted his allegiance and moved next to Jack.

"I was just telling your aunt," said Uncle Fred. "I bumped into Ruan Brock while I was out. He was telling me how some of his sheep had died up there in Oak Field. It seems they just keeled over in the night. You've been up there a lot recently. You haven't seen anything, have you?"

"No!" said Jack," a little abruptly. He was getting a bit fed up with being interrogated about dead sheep. "No, nothing I can think of."

"Oh," said Uncle Fred, a little taken aback by his reply. "Well, never mind, I expect they'll find out what's killing them soon enough."

Aunt Lori brought a plate over with three

sausages and two rounds of bread and butter on it, and put it down in front of Jack. "Don't burn your mouth - they'll be piping hot inside."

Jack picked up the tomato ketchup bottle and squeezed a dollop out on to his plate at the side of his sausages.

"How did you get on with those mirrors?" enquired Uncle Fred. "Did they work?"

"Yes, we could see nearly all the way to the bottom."

"Good. I did a great job on those bricks, even though I do say so myself. It took some time, I can tell you." He got up from the table. "Well, I can't sit here chattering all day, I've got things to do." He walked away from the table and then turned around. "Oh, I nearly forgot. I could do with your help with the flagpole tomorrow. It needs re-painting, and it's about time I looked at those gears. Are you going to be around?"

"Yeah, probably," said Jack.

"Good."

11

"Careful," said Uncle Fred, as they lowered the flagpole to the ground, the pole pivoting at the bottom. He had placed an upturned bucket with a rolled-up rag on top at the other side of the path, and they lowered it down to rest on top of it. "Right, let's have a look at those gears," he said, turning his attention to the other end of the pole.

The motor and gears were housed in a wooden box at the base of the pole. He took a screwdriver from his toolbox, unscrewed the side panel and lifted it off, laying it on the ground. The electric motor could be seen at the bottom of the box, sitting on four tall pillars. It had several large cobwebs around it. Uncle Fred brushed them away, and then reached for a tub of grease. Using the end of a screwdriver, he scooped out a few dollops and applied them to the teeth of each of the two big cogs connected to the motor.

"There, that should do it. I'll just run it up to make sure it's fixed it."

He went into the workshop. Jack could see him through the end window. He reached over to the switch at the side of the window, and the motor at the bottom of the flagpole whirred into life. The gears squeaked for a while, and then gradually became quieter as the grease worked its way around them. Uncle Fred switched it off again.

"Sounds as good as new," said Uncle Fred, returning from the workshop. He picked up the side panel and screwed it back on. "OK, now let's have a look at that pole. We need to take the flag rope off first."

The thin rope passed around two pulleys, one at the bottom of the pole and one at the top. The one at the bottom had a small toothed cog bolted to it, which with the pole upright, was turned by the motor. Once the rope was removed, they rubbed the pole down with sandpaper to remove any loose paint. Then, after wiping it down with a damp rag to take off any dust, they applied a coat of shiny white paint.

"There, that looks better," said Uncle Fred, as he covered the last bit with paint. "I don't know about you, but I could do with a cup of tea."

***

Jack thought that as Ryan wasn't going to be around, he would ride into Poldreath to get some more glue. Aunt Lori was busy watering her bonsai trees as he came through the back door. Each tiny, carefully-pruned tree was planted in a shallow dish. They were sitting on the kitchen window-sill, and she was dribbling water into each one from a small copper watering can. Most of the dishes contained just a tree, but others also had little scenes. The largest dish had mountains made of pointed stones and a lake of blue glass. A tiny elm tree had been planted at the side of the lake, and a group of clay figures were sitting beneath its twisting branches, on a lush grass bank made of moss.

"I thought I might cycle over to Poldreath," said Jack.

"All right dear. Oh, you couldn't pop into the newsagents and collect my magazine, could you? It should have been delivered here yesterday – the shop knows all about it. It's all paid for, you just have to ask for it at the till. It's called The Cottage Gardener."

"The Cottage Gardener," repeated Jack. "OK, I'll see what I can do."

Jack opened a tall cupboard next to the back door and took out an old blue rucksack.

"When are you walking Cody?" asked his

aunt. "I'm not going to walk him, not when you're on holiday. I get enough of that during term time."

"I shouldn't be long. I'll walk him when I get back."

Collecting his bike from the garage, he set off down Carey Lane. When he got to Merry Lane, he turned down a narrow, gravelled path which cut through the fields to the cliff top and joined the coastal path that would take him to Poldreath. The path meandered to and fro, following the wrinkles in the cliff top. A little further on he stopped and rested on a bench overlooking the sea. Kittiwakes were calling out as they flew back and forth to their nests perched high up in the cliff face, and Jack wondered why they would choose to live in such a perilous place. The sun was obscured by a dense blanket of white cloud, but it was still warm, and he was glad of the cool breeze blowing in from the sea. He climbed back onto his bike and carried on to Poldreath.

The coastal path finished at the side of Poldreath Golf Club, and the way down into the town was across one of the fairways that ran along parallel to the cliffs. Jack waited patiently for a group of three golfers to pass by. It seemed to him that he might be putting one of them off, as the man kept hacking at the ball, making it jump into the air and roll to a stop. Jack watched, trying to keep a straight face, as the man slowly progressed down the edge of the fairway in hops, mumbling to himself after each shot.

After a while the fairway was clear, and he walked his bike across and joined the narrow winding path down into the town.

The path squeezed its way between the shops at the bottom to join the High Street. Walking from the quiet cliff top into the busy and noisy centre of Poldreath always seemed strange to Jack, as if he had arrived from another world.

He decided to collect Aunt Lori's magazine from the newsagents first, in case he forgot later. After chaining and locking his bike to a rail at the front, he went inside and joined the short queue for the till. The woman in front of him was wearing a red coat and had a small boy with her. The queue moved forward and she tugged the youngster over to the counter. The boy looked fed up, and kicked the metal foot plate of the counter as she paid for her newspaper. She looked down and saw what he was doing, then tugged him towards the door, telling him off. Jack took his place at the counter.

"I've come to collect my aunt's magazine," he said to the girl behind the counter, who had freckles and long dark hair.

"What's your aunt's name?" she asked.

"Robins," said Jack. "Mrs Robins."

The assistant looked under the counter. "Ah yes, I have it here. The Cottage Gardener."

"Yes, that's it," said Jack.

"If you could just put your name here," she said, placing a piece of paper on the counter in front of him and pointing to the bottom of the page.

Jack signed and took the magazine from her, thanking her.

When he came out of the newsagents the woman in the red coat was talking to a man wearing a green jacket, scruffy blue jeans, and mud-splattered wellingtons. They were standing at the side of his bike. As he walked towards it, they shuffled along the front of the shop to make a space for him, and then continued their conversation.

"According to Willocks up at the garage, it all started over at Port Marron," said the man in a deep gravelly voice.

Jack took his rucksack off, slid the magazine into it, and then dropped it down at the side of his bike. He then bent over the front wheel and pretended to fiddle with the lock, so that he could listen in on the conversation.

"I heard there were some cows over Wanebridge way as well," said the woman. "What do you think's killing them?"

"I don't know," said the man. "But it seems to be covering a lot of ground, so it's not likely to be a dog – unless it's a stray of course."

The boy pulled on the woman's arm. "Can we go now?" he moaned.

She scowled and looked down at him. "In a minute, I'm talking to Ben."

"I've been lucky so far," the man said, "none of my livestock have been affected."

The boy pulled on the woman's arm again. "Yes, all right, all right! Anyway, it's nice to see you again, Ben. Say hello to Jenny for me." With that she walked away. The man walked past Jack, who was pretending he'd only just managed to unlock his bike, and entered the newsagents. Jack headed off towards the model shop.

Blackwell's was tucked away amongst houses down one of the back streets. It was an Aladdin's cave, its shelves stacked high with all sorts of model kits. Planes and helicopters hung from the ceiling. There were several tall hexagonal glass cabinets displaying the latest models, all assembled and painted to perfection by Mr Blackwell. Jack hadn't been there for some time, so he had a good look around. Some of the models were new. One was a Chinook, a big long helicopter with double rotors. He thought he might have a go at making it next. But it was expensive, and he didn't have enough money with him to buy it today.

He walked towards the back of the shop, picked out the bottles of glue he needed and took them to the till.

"I haven't seen you for a while," said Mr Blackwell, a tall thin man with a short stubby brown beard and an easy-going manner.

"No, I've been busy building the Lancaster."

"Ah, yes I remember you buying it. How's it going?"

"I've nearly finished it," said Jack.

"Good," said Mr Blackwell. "I see you're needing more glue – uses a lot that one, as I recall."

"Yes, it does," said Jack. He paid for the glue, and said goodbye to Mr Blackwell.

12

Jack made his way back through the town and up to the coastal path. He had been cycling along it for a while, and was getting close to home, when he saw two figures on bikes coming towards him. As they drew nearer, he was dismayed to see that it was Ethan and Neil. With the cliff on one side and a fenced field on the other, there was nowhere for him to go. He carried on, keeping his head down in the hope that they wouldn't recognise him.

But he was out of luck. When they were near enough for him to hear their tyres crunching on the path and were about to pass, Ethan swerved in front of him, blocking his way. Neil swiftly braked and came to a stop behind him.

"Going somewhere?" asked Ethan.

Jack thought it was a stupid question, since that was obvious. He felt like saying that yes, he had been going somewhere until Ethan had blocked his way, but decided against it, as that would only wind him up.

"Home," he said.

"Oh, that's nice," said Ethan. "I'm glad I bumped into you. I wanted to say sorry for kicking over your bike the other day."

Jack couldn't believe his own ears. Was he actually apologising?

"No. It's a such great bike, it would have been a shame to break it. What I should have done is done a deal with you. Your bike for my bike. After all, mine's much better than yours."

Jack was horrified. His bike wasn't new — about five years old — but he kept it looking like new, hosing it down when it got muddy and touching up any stone chips so that its burnt orange and silver paintwork was almost spotless. Ethan's bike, on the other hand, was so badly beaten up and rusty you could hardly tell what colour it was meant to be.

"I'm fine thanks," said Jack.

"But I'm giving you this great bike of mine in exchange for yours."

"Nah," said Jack, seeing Ethan wasn't going to take no for an answer. "You're all right, I think I'll stick with mine thanks."

"But I insist," said Ethan, reaching over and grabbing hold of Jack's handlebars.

But Jack was ready for him. He quickly twisted the handlebars around, forcing Ethan to let go and tipping him over sideways. He then lifted his front wheel out of the way of Ethan's, and took off, pedalling as fast as he could. By the time Ethan had regained his balance, he had built up quite a lead.

"I'M GOING TO GET YOU FOR THAT!" screamed Ethan, spinning his bike around and setting off after him.

"YOU CAN'T GET AWAY FROM ME!" yelled Ethan, who was slowly gaining on him.

Jack couldn't pedal any faster. He tried, but each time his feet slipped off the pedals and he lost speed. He was wondering what else he could do to escape when he heard a scream behind him. He glanced over his shoulder. Ethan was lying flat out on the path, his bike lying on its side in front of him. Jack slammed on his brakes and brought his bike around, then flicked his hair out of his eyes. Ethan turned over and sat up, hugging his knees. He got back to his feet, and brushed himself down. Neil, who hadn't been so quick off the mark, pulled up alongside him and Ethan started waving his arms around, pointing at the path behind them and shouting at him as if it was his fault that he'd fallen off. He looked around and saw Jack watching him, hollered something in his direction, and then picked up his bike and started pedalling frantically towards him again, his face flushed with renewed anger.

Jack turned away, and was about to hop back onto his saddle when he heard another scream. He looked around just in time to see Ethan's bike leave the path and crash into the fence. But Ethan was nowhere to be seen. The cry had come from above. He looked up. What the...? Ethan was up in the air, dangling in space, his legs kicking about wildly and moving towards the edge of the cliff. Just as he reached the edge he fell to the ground, staggered sideways, and disappeared from view. Neil dropped his bike and ran over to the spot.

Jack was torn between the instinct to ride away while he still had the chance and his desire to see what had happened to Ethan. His curiosity won. Propping his bike up against a fence post in case he needed to make a quick getaway, he ran over to the place where Ethan had vanished – and recognised it immediately. It was the section of cliff with the hollow and the hole leading down to the cave. Neil was standing at the edge of the hollow with his mouth wide open looking down at Ethan, whose bottom half had disappeared down the hole.

"Don't stand there gawping," shouted Ethan. "Get me out of here!"

Neil snapped out of his stupor and jumped down into the hollow. Slipping his arms around Ethan's chest under his armpits, he heaved with all his might. He tried again and again to lift him out the hole, steadily going more red in the face, but couldn't shift him. He looked towards Jack for help.

Jack was considering whether to help him when he heard words again inside his head – Arkus.

Do not help him. For this to work they must think that you are the one doing these things.

"It was you!" gasped Jack.

Yes, I have returned to size. Say this to the one that you call Ethan – If you promise to stop bothering me, I will get you out.

"If you promise to stop bothering me, I'll get you out," said Jack.

Ethan looked straight at him, wide eyed. "What did you say?"

"I said, if you promise to stop bothering me, I'll get you out of there."

"Yeah, right. Like you could get me out. I don't know what's going on here, but there's no way you..." He stopped talking abruptly, changing his mind. "Okay then, I promise."

"You promise to leave me alone from now on," said Jack.

"Yeah... Yeah, I promise."

"That goes for him as well," said Jack, nodding towards Neil.

"Yeah, he'll leave you alone as well."

Tell the other one to stand back, said Arkus.

"Neil, come out of there," said Jack.

Neil looked at Ethan for his approval and then climbed out, moving away from the edge, and keeping his distance from Jack.

Now hold out your hand towards him and raise it slowly, said Arkus.

Jack did as instructed. He heard the sound of giant wings beating, and then felt the air swirl around him. Pinch marks appeared on the shoulders of Ethan's brown leather jacket as Arkus grasped him in his claws. "Whoa – what's happening?" cried Ethan.

Jack raised his right hand and Ethan rose up into the air. When he was clear of the hole, he floated magically across to the far side of the hollow.

Now lower it again, instructed Arkus.

Jack lowered his hand and Ethan floated down to the ground, landing on his feet. He glared across at Jack from the other side of the hollow. "What's going on here?" he demanded.

"I just got you out," said Jack. "Now, you've got to keep your side of the bargain, and leave me alone."

"And what are you gonna do if I don't?" sneered Ethan.

Arkus spoke again. *I believe this one needs another lesson. Say 'this'.*

"This," repeated Jack.

Ethan suddenly doubled up and flew

backwards through the air, landing in the grass on his back. He sat up grimacing, clenching his stomach, and was immediately whisked backwards up into the air over the edge of the cliff. Now dangling some way out, like a puppet with most of its strings cut, his face turned white as he stared down with horror at the beach below.

Hold your hand out again, said Arkus. *Tell him that the next time he pesters you, you will drop him.*

Jack did as he said, making a clenched fist as if he was holding on to Ethan.

Ethan turned shakily towards him. "OK, OK... d... don't drop me!"

"You won't pester me ever again," said Jack.

"No, I... I swear, I swear," said Ethan.

"All right," said Jack, who was beginning to get the hang of his new power. Without any further instruction from Arkus he began to bring his hand back round towards the land. At that moment there was a loud shriek. Jack peered over the edge of the cliff, and saw a figure on the path down to the beach.

"Someone's coming," said Jack.

I see them, came Arkus' reply.

Arkus dropped Ethan down on to the cliff top, where he lay in a crumpled heap.

"Now get out of here!" shouted Jack.

Ethan scrambled to his feet and ran towards his bike. Neil looked nervously across at Jack, obviously trying to decide if it was safe to move, and then ran after Ethan.

Jack ran over to retrieve his bike. As he reached for the handlebars, he heard someone call out his name.

"Jack, stop!"

He turned around to see Kerra striding purposefully towards him. "What's going on? I saw th, th, that boy," she said, stammering and pointing at Ethan, who was pedalling away from them at speed. He was j, j, just hanging in the air over the cliff."

"I didn't see anything," said Jack, innocently.

"You must have!" said Kerra. "You were pointing at him."

Jack decided there was nothing for it; he would have to tell Kerra the truth. "All right, I'll tell you. He was pestering me, so I was teaching him a lesson."

"Yeah, right."

"I was. But I had some help."

"What do you mean?" demanded Kerra.

"If you hang on a minute, I'll show you," said Jack.

Jack looked up. "Arkus, I need you to show yourself." Arkus didn't reply.

"Who are you talking to?" asked Kerra.

Jack tried again. "Arkus, please prove that you exist to this girl."

Are you sure that is wise? asked Arkus.

"Yes, I'm sure," said Jack.

Very well. This girl - she is called Kerra?

"Yes."

Arkus spoke softly so as not to startle her. *Kerra.*

She jerked her head round. "Who said that?"

Do not be alarmed. My name is Arkus.

"What? Where are you?"

Part of the low wooden fence at the side of the path shattered, sending splinters of wood into the air, making them both jump.

Sorry. I am... here.

"This is the one who helped me," said Jack.

"But what is it?" asked Kerra.

"That may take a while to explain," said Jack. "Let's sit down."

They sat down on the grass at the side of the path, and Jack told her about all the strange things that had been happening.

"So, this other creature, this Torg, is what you were running away from when I saw you the other day?" asked Kerra, when he'd finished.

"Yes."

"I thought there was something funny going on there," said Kerra.

Arkus materialised close to where they were sitting. He was lying on his front, and was now the size of an elephant, his large head looming over them.

"Whoa," cried Jack, staring up at him, "I had no idea how big – so this is your normal size?"

It is, replied Arkus.

There was a gash near the end of his tail, which had purple blood seeping from it.

"You're hurt," said Jack.

Yes.

"Did you just cut that on the fence?"

No, I used it to stop that unusual-looking machine the boy Ethan was riding. But do not worry, it will heal quickly.

"Do you think Ethan will leave you alone now?" asked Kerra.

"Yeah. You know, somehow, I think he will."

"So how do we stop this creature?" asked Kerra.

A good question, said Arkus.

"Did you manage to track it down?" asked Jack.

I do not know its exact location. It went deep under the ground and I lost track of it. Arkus lifted up the arm with the gold band. *I am afraid my armlet has limited powers.*

"I can see it underground," said Jack. "We could help you."

Then perhaps with your help we may find it again.

"Yeah," said Jack, excitedly. Then he remembered his bike. "But what about my bike? I can't leave it here."

"You could leave it at the farm," said Kerra. "Then Arkus could meet us at the bottom of Oak Field."

"Yeah, that'd work," said Jack.

Then I shall see you shortly, said Arkus.

He pressed the gold band around his arm, and promptly disappeared. Moments later they heard a drumming on the grass nearby, followed by the slow, rhythmic beat of giant wings as he took to the sky.

Jack and Kerra carried on along the cliff top path to the farm, Jack pushing his bike along beside him. "So, what were you doing down on the beach?" he asked.

"Oh, I often go down there. There are some

amazing rock pools. I found a shark in one once. It was really pretty, a sort of creamy white colour with pale brown spots."

"Really, how big?"

"Oh, only small, a bit bigger than my hand. It was just sitting there under the seaweed looking at me. I looked it up when I got home. It was a cat shark."

"I take Cody down there sometimes," said Jack.

"Who's Cody, your dog?"

"Yeah, a black Lab," said Jack. "It's tricky taking him rock pooling though, he always jumps in and stirs up the water, scaring everything away. When I go with Ryan, we usually take it in turns to hold on to his lead, so one of us can look in the pools without him barging in and spoiling things."

They arrived at the farm.

"Your bike should be safe over there," said Kerra, pointing down the side of a long black barn.

Jack wheeled his bike down the side of the

barn and leant it against the wall. Then they made their way back over to Oak Field, and waited for Arkus.

13

Arkus landed near the gate, creating four flat patches in the grass with his feet. *Climb on my back,* he told Jack.

Jack walked towards him until his legs bumped up against something soft. He took hold of a handful of Arkus' fur and hauled himself up.

"You just disappeared," cried Kerra.

He reached down and touched her wrist, making her jump. "Here – I'll help you up."

Kerra took his hand, and pulled herself up on to Arkus' back, and then they shuffled along until they were sitting astride his neck. Jack was sitting in front, a little way back from his head, with Kerra behind him.

Arkus took several giant strides and took to the air. They quickly gained height, and swept around away from the coast. Being so high with the wind buffeting against them was both exhilarating and scary all at the same time. Arkus' neck moved up and down beneath them as he beat his giant wings, and if they hadn't been holding on tight, they could easily have fallen off. Jack saw Carey Lane and the house off to the right, and wondered what his aunt and uncle were doing, and what they would think if they knew he was flying high in the sky sitting astride Arkus.

As they approached a gently-sloping grassy field with a small patch of trees at the top, Arkus spoke again.

It was here that I saw it last – at the edge of those trees. It was moving towards one of those silvery towers. What are they?

Jack looked down and saw a line of

electricity pylons at the far side of the field.
"They're pylons," he said. "They carry power
cables from the power stations to the villages
and towns. The power is at a dangerously
high voltage, so they put them up high, out
of harm's way."

And this power moves along these... these
cables on its own?

"Eh, yes," answered Jack, thinking it a
strange question.

As they flew nearer the pylons, Jack thought
he saw something. "There's something down
there near the bottom of the field," he said.

Arkus pressed a section of the gold band
around his arm. *I am not getting anything.*

"Maybe the cables are shielding it," said
Jack. "Can you take us down a little?"

Arkus took them lower. They were now
flying down the hill alongside the high voltage
cables.

"There!" shouted Jack. "See it – under those
cables."

Kerra leant towards him and shouted into

his ear. "Where, I can't see it?"

"There, near that pylon at the bottom of the hill."

The bumps on the Torg were flickering, creating bands of red that travelled down its body. It came out from under the cables.

"I see it," shrieked Kerra. "It's sort of red."

Ah, said Arkus, inspecting his bracelet again, *I have it now. Hold on tight both of you.*

He flew down under the power cables and out over a neighbouring field, then climbing higher, swept back around towards the Torg. When he was almost on top of it, he turned in the air, sweeping his wings upwards, dropping down on to it and grasping it in his claws. The Torg was caught off guard. It let out an ear-piercing screech as Arkus' claws dug into its back. Arkus held on tight as it twisted and turned, trying to escape his grasp. It suddenly changed direction, doubling back on itself, and tore itself from his grip, plunging back into the ground.

Arkus made several slightly wobbly strides

and took to the air. *I fear it is becoming more powerful. I wish the Garner Ray was operational so that we could finish this once and for all.* He flew back around over the same spot.

"I can't see it anywhere," said Jack.

"Nor can I," said Kerra. "It's vanished."

I believe it has gone deep underground again, said Arkus. He looked up at the sky. It was getting late. *I think I had best take you back.*

After dropping Jack and Kerra off at the bottom of Oak Field, Arkus took to the air again.

"When do you think we'll see him again?" asked Kerra, as they walked towards the gate in the corner.

"I don't know," said jack. "I suppose It depends on when the Torg comes back up to the surface."

"Arkus said it had gone deeper. If it can move along down there as easily as it does near the surface it could come up anywhere," said Kerra.

"Hopefully, Arkus will be able to detect it."

"As long as it's not hiding under those high voltage cables again."

"Yeah, providing it's not under those. Although he knows to look under them now."

They arrived at the farm, and walked through the gate to retrieve Jack's bike.

"Who's this then?" said a deep voice from inside the barn.

"Oh, Dad. I didn't see you there," said Kerra. "This is Jack."

Mr Brock came out from the barn, wiping his hands on a rag. He was wearing a blue boiler suit smeared with oil. He was stocky with a round face, which broke into a large smile.

"Ah, yes of course, young Jack," he said. "You've grown a bit since I saw you last."

"You two know each other?" said Kerra, giving Jack a cold stare for not mentioning he knew her father.

"Yes, Jack sometimes helps out his aunt at the Country Fair – she has a bonsai display there. And his Uncle Fred comes here sometimes – he's a dab hand at repairing things." Mr Brock turned to Jack. "I take it you'll be at the fair again this year? We'll be holding it in Marley Field. It's less boggy, and I've got cattle on the main one."

"I think my aunt's planning to be there," said Jack, trying to avoid Kerra's unnerving stare.

"Great. Well I must get on. Probably see you at the fair." And with that he turned and walked back into the barn, disappearing into the gloomy interior.

"Why didn't you tell me you knew my dad?" asked Kerra.

"It never came up," said Jack. "Anyway, I didn't think it was important."

"Humph!" said Kerra. "So, what is it that you do at the fair exactly?"

"I just help out – carrying stuff mostly." He glanced at his watch. "Look, I think I'd better be going, they'll be wondering where I've got to. I'll see you around – maybe at the fair."

***

Aunt Lori was at the kitchen sink, and she soon spotted Jack slinking in through the back door. "Where have you been?" she asked.

Jack quickly thought up a good excuse. "I was up at the crater. I left there a while ago, and I was on my way home when Ruan Brock collared me. He wanted to know if we were going to the Country Fair this year."

Aunt Lori scowled, not at all impressed by his excuse. "Hmmm. Well, I walked Cody, since you weren't around. What about my magazine – did you get that?"

"Oh yeah, it's in here," said Jack, swinging the rucksack down off his shoulder. He took the magazine out and handed it to her.

"Thank you," said Aunt Lori.

"Ruan said the fair was going to be in Marley Field this year."

Uncle Fred was sitting at the kitchen table, and looked up from his newspaper. "It must

be our turn again then. It doesn't seem like
two years since we held it here last."

14

Jack was perched on the edge of his seat at his desk. He was assembling some of the larger parts of the Lancaster, holding one of the tail fins in one hand and the fuselage in the other. He carefully lined them up, and then brought the two parts together. He was thinking about the Torg and where it might have gone. Arkus had said they had several months before it became powerful enough to kill them. But how were they going to destroy it? It seemed to have so easily escaped their attack. What if they *couldn't* destroy it?

The front door bell rang, and he heard talking downstairs.

"Ryan's here," called Aunt Lori, letting him in through the door. "He's upstairs in his room, Ryan."

"You all right?" enquired Ryan, seeing Jack crouched over the desk.

"Yeah, I can't let go of this until the glue takes hold."

Ryan walked over and plonked himself down on the end of the bed. "What's been happening here then, has Arkus come back?"

Jack told Ryan how they'd tracked down and attacked the Torg.

"Wow, sounds like it was quite a fight. I think we ought to tell someone about the Torg."

"Who?"

"I don't know. The police I suppose?"

"I don't think they'd believe us," said Jack, "We've got nothing to show them. We can't even prove it exists." He inspected the new part. "I'll leave that to glue a bit longer before

I stick the other tail fin on." He got up from his chair. Cody noticed him moving and rose from his basket. He stretched, tilting his head back, looking up at Jack expectantly.

"I think he needs a walk," said Jack.

"I don't think Ethan will be bothering us any more," said Jack, as they were walking down Carey Lane, Cody pulling eagerly on his lead in front.

"Why, has something happened to him?" asked Ryan.

"Sort of," said Jack. He described how Arkus had dangled Ethan over the edge of the cliff.

"He thinks you've got special powers," said Ryan.

"I know," said Jack, grinning and nodding. "Isn't it great?"

"I wish I'd been there to see the look on his face when you had him dangling over the cliff."

"Yeah, you really missed something. So, how did the fishing go?"

"It was great. I caught a bass."

"A big one?"

"Yeah," said Ryan, taking out his phone. He moved his finger across the screen and showed Jack a photo of him proudly cradling a huge fish.

"Whoa," said Jack. "Where did you catch it?"

"Just off the Seven Sisters, over towards the entrance to the harbour. We'd been out to sea and not had so much as a nibble. The captain thought it might be worth trying there on the way back."

"Must have been tricky to bring in."

"Yeah, it was," said Ryan. "It fought like a pig. Weighed in at ten pounds."

"You catch anything else?"

"I didn't, but my dad caught a small wrasse."

They returned from walking Cody and let him off his lead. He ambled into the house, where they could hear him lapping from his water bowl.

Uncle Fred came limping down the garden path towards them. "Hello you two. I've just been checking on the flagpole. I think it's ready to go up again - if you're feeling strong."

They followed him down the garden. He was walking quite briskly despite his injured leg, hobbling along steadily in front of them.

"If you two can lift it, I'll make sure the gears mesh correctly," said Uncle Fred, moving towards the other end of the flag pole.

They lifted the pole, slowly working their way towards the bottom end. Then, holding it high above their heads, they pushed it up into its upright position.

"The gears seemed to have meshed all right," said Uncle Fred, "but we'd better check to see it all works." He disappeared off to the workshop, and came back a moment later carrying the skull and cross bones flag. He clipped it on to the rope at the bottom, and then went back into the workshop. The motor sprung to life, and the flag rose smoothly and quietly up the pole. Catching the wind at the top, it unfurled, the skull moving ominously as it waved to and fro.

15

The Country Fair was the highlight of the
year. It was such a big event that it was
shared between the villages of Port Marron
and Kerstle, each village holding it on
alternate years. This year it was to be held
in Port Marron. It was an overcast day, with
hardly any wind. Jack was travelling to the
fair in a big, old and rather tatty estate car
with his aunt and uncle. The luggage area
behind the back seats was packed with boxes
of Aunt Lori's bonsai trees.

Cody was sitting on the back seat next to

Jack. As they arrived at the exhibitors' gate, he jumped up to the side window and started barking.

Jack pulled him down by his collar. "Shh Cody!"

Uncle Fred pulled into the gate, and then wound down the window. A man dressed in a bright orange 'Country Fair' T-shirt came over to talk to them.

"We're displaying in the craft marquee," said Uncle Fred.

"Ah, you'll want to follow the blue arrows round to the right," said the man. "You should be able to park just behind the marquee to unload. Once you've done that, move your car over to the exhibitor's car park, which you'll find over on the left-hand side there."

"Thank you," said Uncle Fred.

The craft marquee was a long tent with a door at each end, and it housed eight tables, four down each side.

Jack helped carry the boxes of bonsai in from the car. "Where do you want these?"

"Oh, put them down there on the floor," said Aunt Lori, standing behind the table that had been reserved for them. "I can sort out where they're going later."

She had tied Cody to one of the rear table legs and placed an old blanket on the floor for him to lie on. On hearing Jack's voice, he stuck his head out of the side, pushing the dark green cloth that covered the table up with his nose.

Jack bent down and ruffled his fur. "You all right under there Cody?"

He fetched the last box in from the car, putting it down on the floor with the others. "That's all of them. Uncle Fred's gone to move the car. Is it all right if I go and look around now?"

"Yes. I think I can see Ryan over there."

"Where?"

"Over there, at the other end of the tent."

"Oh yeah."

"Could you take Cody with you? He could do with stretching his legs.

"Oh, I was going to do the fair," said Jack.

"Well, let him have a bit of a walk, and then bring him back," said Aunt Lori.

Jack undid Cody's lead from around the table leg, and Cody licked him. "I'll see you in a bit then," he said.

The tables were slowly filling with all kinds of crafts. The next table along had a variety of brightly-coloured plates, pots and jugs on display, and a woman was busy setting up a potter's wheel to one side, to show how it was done. A multitude of stained-glass plaques filled the next table, some hanging from shelves at each side. Mrs Gainer's table was near the door at the end, and had been covered in a powder blue cloth. Ryan was busy placing eagle carvings out along the front, like the one his mother had given to Jack.

He looked up. "Ah, great, you made it."

"Are you here with your aunt?" asked Mrs Gainer, looking over from the back of the table.

"Yeah. She's just setting up down at the other end of the tent."

"Great, I'll go over and have a chat later."

"Can I go now?" asked Ryan.

"In a minute. Can you give me a hand with this elephant first? It wants to go in that corner."

This was the carving Jack had seen next to the door in the studio. Ryan and his mum picked it up from the floor and placed it down on the table. It was only for show, as it had a label around its neck saying 'NOT FOR SALE.'

"There, that looks right," said Mrs Gainer, after shuffling it around a little. "Okay, you can go now."

There was music playing over the speakers of the public address system, occasionally interrupted by an exceedingly cheerful man giving out information on up and coming events. "... and the sheep shearing over on the far side of the main arena is due to start shortly," he said.

"Let's make our way over there," said Jack, "we might see Kerra."

They passed the end of a short queue leading into the food and drink marquee, a large tent with a mixture of sausages, onions, cheese, burgers and curry smells wafting out from it, and Jack had to pull Cody away from it.

The sheep shearing was at the edge of the field, and a crowd had formed along the metal barrier at the front. Jack didn't want to take Cody too near in case he upset the sheep, so they stood over to one side, behind a line of people. Kerra was leading out one of the sheep from its pen, shuffling it along between her legs. It didn't want to come out, and kept backing up, making her stagger backwards. Mr Brock appeared from the rear of a van at the side of the enclosure. He hopped over the barrier to help her, and they led it over to the shearing area, which was behind the barrier at the front. He swapped positions with her, and then deftly flipped the sheep over on to its back, ready for shearing.

Jack waved to Kerra to get her attention. "Kerra, over here!"

Ducking under the barrier at the side, she worked her way through the crowd to join them.

"Hi."

"You seemed to be struggling a bit there," said Jack.

"Oh, they're not normally that bad," said Kerra. "It's because they're in an unfamiliar place."

She saw Cody laying at Jack's feet, and squatted down to pat him. "So, this is Cody. Are you entering him into any of the dog obedience competitions?"

"He doesn't really do obedience," said Jack.

"Oh, that's a shame," said Kerra. "I'd enter one of our two, but they're both working dogs, and they're not allowed in."

Mr Brock finished shearing, and the shorn sheep, much thinner now, leapt to its feet. He held up the fleece, which he'd managed to shave off in one piece, and everyone clapped.

"I'd better be going," said Kerra, standing up. "But someone else is taking over my job after lunch, so I should be free then."

"OK we'll come by a bit later," said Jack.

Jack and Ryan carried on looking around. Screams and whoops of laughter were coming from the fairground in the neighbouring field. There was a tall hedgerow separating the fields, and a big wheel was slowly spinning around above it, its bright coloured lights contrasting with the dull grey sky.

"I'll drop Cody back with my aunt later on and then we can do the fair," said Jack.

The rare breeds pens were surrounded by young children, as was the Punch and Judy show, which was in full swing, with Punch's squeaks breaking through the general hubbub of the fair. They came to a display of cars, each one highly polished and in pristine condition. The sports cars along the front were modern, but behind them was a row of older cars. Jack saw one that looked the same as his uncle's and walked over to it.

"This is the same as ours," he said, peering in through the driver's window. "Maybe we ought to park ours here."

"I think your car needs a lot of work done on it before you could display it here," said Ryan.

"I suppose we'd have to get some of the dents out first," said Jack, grinning.

"Yeah, and all the rust."

16

After grabbing a burger at a nearby stall, they made their way over to the craft marquee. Jack gave his last bit of burger to Cody at the tent door. Aunt Lori was busy showing someone her collection of bonsai. Jack tied Cody's lead around the table leg and he sank down on to his rug. Uncle Fred had found himself a chair and was dozing in the corner with part of a newspaper on his lap, the rest having fallen off on to the ground. Jack waved his arms to get Aunt Lori's attention, and then pointed to Cody, and she smiled back.

Jack and Ryan were making their way back over to the shearing display when someone called out, "Oi, careful! You nearly had me over then."

Jack looked around to an enormous pair of stripy black and white trousers. He craned his neck up to see a heavily-painted man wearing an orange wig and a green clown's costume. He was standing on stilts.

"Sorry, I didn't see you," said Jack.

The man was bending over slightly, making tiny steps with the stilts, backwards and forwards, trying to regain his balance. In a few moments he had sorted himself out, and stood up straight. "That's all right. No harm done." He lifted up a leg, took a giant step and lurched off down the field.

"He came out of nowhere," said Jack. "I didn't see him."

"No, me neither," said Ryan.

Kerra had finished her shift. "I was just coming to look for you. What took you so long?"

"I was almost mown down by some giant maniac," said Jack.

"What?"

"Some clown on stilts," said Ryan.

"Oh yes, I've seen him going round," said Kerra. "I think there's some sort of circus school on the other side of the field. Where do you want to go?"

"We haven't been to the fair yet," said Ryan.

"What about the big wheel?" suggested Jack. "We can talk without being overheard up there."

After waiting in the queue and paying, they took up their seats inside one of the cages, with Jack sitting next to Ryan and Kerra on the seat opposite. The big wheel moved around slowly, stopping every now and again to let on more people. It came to a stop near the top, rocking gently backwards and forwards.

When it stopped rocking, Kerra shuffled forward in her seat. "So, what's been happening? Have you heard anything from Arkus?"

"No, nothing," said Jack. "It's all gone quiet."

"I think we ought to tell the police," said Kerra.

"That's what I said," said Ryan.

"Yes, but I don't think they'd believe us. We've got nothing to show them."

"What about those burn marks up at the crater?" said Kerra. "We could show them those."

"Yeah, what about those?" asked Ryan.

"They're a bit strange I agree, but it's not enough. They're not going to take us seriously, without more proof."

"No, I suppose not," said Kerra.

"The only thing we could do is ask Arkus to show himself," said Jack, "but I don't think he'd agree. We know he's harmless, but other people might see him as a danger, and have him locked up, or set the army on him. I don't know about you, but I couldn't ask him to do that."

The cage started down and they sat quietly, each in their own thoughts, gazing out over the fair and the surrounding countryside.

Jack suddenly sat bolt upright. "The Torg! It's over there, at the edge of the field!"

"I can't see anything," said Kerra.

"It's probably under the ground," said Ryan. "Jack's the only one who can see it underground. I think it must have been that bump to his head."

"What bump?" asked Kerra.

"Never mind about that," said Jack. "I'll tell you later. I think it's coming this way."

Jack watched the Torg pass below them into the main field. Studying it closely, he thought it looked bigger.

"Where is it now?" asked Ryan.

"In the main field," said Jack. "NO!"

"What is it?" asked Kerra.

"It's closing in on that man – the one on stilts. We need to get down there."

It seemed like an age before their cage stopped at the bottom. Jumping out, they hurried over to the main field. The stilt man was lying on his back on the ground, the Torg sitting under him. A small group of people had noticed him, and were going over to help.

STAND BACK! It was Arkus, but this time everyone could hear his voice. The group stopped walking and looked around, trying to work out where the shout had come from. Seconds later two large holes appeared at the side of the stricken man, as Arkus drove his feet into the ground. Alarmed by the sudden disturbance, the Torg moved away, heading back towards the edge of the field. Two first aiders from the St John's Ambulance tent arrived, and rushed over to help the man. They knelt down next to him, one of them cradling his head. As Jack, Ryan and Kerra stood watching they heard a voice behind them.

"I wonder if I could have a word?"

They turned around to see PC Harkin walking briskly towards them.

He looked straight at Jack.

"You again. Why is it when anything happens around here, you're always somewhere in the vicinity?" He turned to Ryan. "The same applies to you."

Before Jack or Ryan could answer, Kerra spoke up. "We'd be glad to help you with your enquires officer," she said, smiling.

"Aren't you Mr Brock's daughter?" said PC Harkin.

"Yes, my name's Kerra."

"Well Kerra, perhaps you'd like to explain why you were all running over here from that Ferris wheel a minute ago?"

"We saw that poor man fall off his stilts," said Kerra.

"And we were going over to see if we could help him," interjected Jack.

PC Harkin eyed them both suspiciously, and then pointed to the Big Wheel. "You saw him fall off from all the way up there?"

"Yes," said Jack, "I just happened to be looking in that direction."

"You just happened to be looking in that

direction," repeated PC Harkin. He turned to Ryan. "You're very quiet."

"No, that's exactly what happened," said Ryan.

"Hmmm," said PC Harkin, frowning. "Well it all looked very suspicious to me. I can't see why you'd be so worried about a man falling off his stilts – worried enough, that is, to come running all the way over here."

"We know him," said Jack. Which was sort of true, since he'd spoken to him less than an hour ago.

"Hmmm," sighed PC Harkin. "Well I still think it's strange." He took out his notebook and started writing in it. He carried on writing for some time, and seemed to have forgotten they were there.

"Er... can we go now?" asked Jack.

PC Harkin looked up, and waved his pencil. "Yes, yes off you go."

They left PC Harkin scribbling in his notebook.

Arkus spoke to them as they were walking away. *We need to talk. If you go over to the far corner of the other field, I'll join you.*

The fair was winding down as people began to leave, the big wheel now standing still. As they got to the far corner, they heard Arkus land nearby. They watched the grass mysteriously flatten in his footsteps as he walked towards them.

It almost killed that man, said Arkus. *It is maturing much faster than I expected. We only have days before it becomes too strong for me to defeat it. We must lure it to the surface. Kerra, would it be possible to use one of the sheep from your farm?*

"To use as bait?" asked Kerra.

Yes. I will try to keep it safe.

"Isn't there some other way we could lure it up to the surface?" asked Kerra.

No, I am afraid not. The Torg has returned to the crater. It has killed these animals there before. If you bring rope and some kind of stake, we can tether it so it does not wander.

We will make the attack tonight, under cover of darkness. Jack, is there somewhere I can land close to your dwelling?

"At the back of our house," said Jack, "there should be room there."

Then I shall see you two there at sundown.

Tremors ran through the ground as Arkus took to the air. The three of them walked back towards the main field. Kerra turned towards Jack as they were passing through the gap in the hedgerow. "Listen, I need to go and help my dad load up the van. I'll see you both tonight. I think it got dark about nine last night."

"Okay, we'll see you there about nine," said Jack.

Jack and Ryan headed towards the craft marquee.

"Do you think you'll be able to get away by nine o'clock?" asked Jack.

"Yeah, should be okay. I'll tell my mum I'm not feeling well and have an early night, then sneak out later."

Aunt Lori was chatting to Ryan's mother as they entered the marquee. She looked over and smiled.

"Ah, here they are. We were just saying we've not seen you for a while."

Cody shot out from under the table to greet them, jolting it and making the bonsai trees shake as if there had been a tiny bonsai-sized earthquake.

"Did you miss me then?" said Jack, bending down and patting him.

Mrs Gainer smiled. "Well, we'd better be getting on. There's still a lot to do. It's been lovely catching up with you again."

17

Back at the house, Jack helped with unloading the car, carrying the boxes of bonsais into the house and placing them down at the far end of the kitchen table, where Aunt Lori had put down sheets of newspaper. After tea, during which he tentatively picked at a ham sandwich, he said he was feeling tired and went up to his room. He opened the bedroom window a crack so he could hear Ryan when he arrived, and then crawled into bed with his clothes on, with just his head poking out of the blankets.

When Aunt Lori came in later on to check he was all right, he pretended to be asleep. Being so warm and comfortable he was finding it hard not to fall asleep for real, so he shuffled up against the headboard and waited for Ryan to arrive, doing his best to stay awake.

"Pssst."

Jack leapt out of bed, pushed the window open, and looked out. It was a clear, almost cloudless night, with a full moon hovering over the conifers down the garden. Ryan was crouching down underneath the kitchen window.

"Hang on, I'm on my way," whispered Jack.

One end of the lean-to was directly below his window. Jack climbed out, sliding down over the window ledge on his stomach until his feet touched the roof. He then shuffled down the glass on his bottom, lowered himself onto the water butt at the side, and jumped to the ground.

"Any sign of Arkus?" he asked, crouching down next to Ryan.

"No, not yet," said Ryan.

After a few minutes they heard the gentle beating of giant wings and Arkus touched down in the middle of the lawn. He was invisible, but they could hear him breathing hard, and see long plumes of moist air escaping from his nostrils.

Climb on, we haven't got much time, he told them.

Jack and Ryan ran across the lawn to his side.

"It's probably easier if I go first," whispered Jack, grabbing hold of Arkus' thick fur. Ryan pulled himself up and sat down behind him. "He moves about a bit," whispered Jack. "so hold tight."

Arkus leapt into the air.

"Whoa!" shouted Ryan as he was tipped backwards, forgetting for a moment that they were trying to be as quiet as possible.

"Shhh!" hissed Jack.

"Sorry," said Ryan.

On reaching the crater Arkus circled overhead, following the outer rim. The Torg was halfway up the side of the hill, next to the path leading up from the gate. There were a dozen or so sheep nearby.

"I don't think this is going to work," said Jack, "it doesn't seem very interested in those sheep. But I have an idea."

Arkus contacted Kerra, and after a short while she appeared at the bottom gate. He spoke to her again, and then landed close by. Jack jumped down.

"Are you sure about this?" she asked. "From what Arkus told me, it could be dangerous."

"Yeah, I'll be fine."

"Well be careful."

Kerra climbed up onto Arkus, sitting down behind Ryan, and Arkus took to the air, spiralling upwards. Jack searched around for a large stone, and then moved further around the hill. He crept up the side until he was standing between the sea and the

Torg, took a deep breath, and then hurled the stone at the patch of ground above it. The stone sailed through the air and landed with a dull thud. The Torg reared up from the ground screeching, dipped back down below the surface, and then came rushing towards him. Jack turned tail and ran, cutting across and down the hill, running at breakneck speed. He glimpsed a rabbit hole in front, and stepped to the side of it just in time, but as he dodged it, the toe of his trainer caught the ground and he stumbled. His arms went out instinctively, flailing around in an effort to arrest his fall. Somehow managing to stay on his feet, he continued on down the side of the hill.

Careful Jack, it is right behind you, said Arkus, following above.

As Jack got closer to the bottom, the ground began to level out. The fence at the edge of the field was coming up fast, and he could see the barbed wire running along the top glinting in the moonlight. Jack took several more strides, pushed down on a fence post and launched himself over it. Landing on the other side, he crossed the path, going as close to the cliff edge as he dared, and then threw himself to the ground.

A split second later, there was a blood-curdling screech as the Torg materialised from the cliff face and tumbled through the air down on to the rocks below, landing with a loud SPLAT.

Arkus landed at his side. *Get on. We must make sure it is dead.*

The Torg had come to a sticky end on the rocks of the promontory. Stretched out in front of them was a large mound of clear jelly, interspersed with red splodges. Some of the jelly was dripping down the side in large globules, hissing as it fell into the rockpools and giving off a strong smell of bad eggs.

"Whoa, that reeks," said Kerra.

"That's the end of that then," said Ryan.

"Good riddance," said Jack. "That thing was evil."

18

Jack's heart was still pounding feverishly in his ears. He hated to think what would have happened if he'd fallen. As he stood looking out to sea, the pounding subsided. The sea was calm with just a gentle swell, the crests of the shallow waves sparkling.

A small fishing vessel appeared around the headland. As it came closer, Jack spotted a red glow near the bow.

"The Torg! It's out there next to that boat."

"It can't be," said Ryan. "It's here, splattered all over these rocks."

Jack looked back at the gooey remains of the Torg. It was obviously completely dead. But how... He looked back at the boat. The red glow was still there. As he returned his gaze to the remains of the Torg he noticed something in the sand, down at the other side of the rocks. There was a large depression with a trail leading down to the sea.

"What's that?"

It is the clone, replied Arkus.

"What?" cried Jack.

Once a Torg has reached maturity it produces a clone, an exact copy of itself. But this Torg is too young, it should not be happening at this time.

A cry rang out from the boat. It was slewing side on, and drifting towards the jagged teeth of the Seven Sisters. As it came around Jack recognised it – the *Blue Angel.*

"Quick!" he said. "We must help."

Arkus and Jack headed out to sea, leaving Ryan and Kerra on top of the promontory.

"If you can hover over the boat, I'll drop

down on board and throw you up a rope," cried Jack.

A few flaps of Arkus' giant wings and they were over the stricken craft. The Torg was circling the boat, the crew lying motionless around the deck. All that is, except Cadan, the captain, whose long thick legs could be seen poking out from the wheelhouse. Jack noticed that the bumps on the Torg were flickering, producing bright red bands that travelled down its body.

Arkus made a second pass, coming in lower and hovering over the boat. Jack jumped down onto the deck and ran over to the rope that he knew would be coiled up at the front, near the prow. Picking up one end, he quickly made an oversized knot. The Torg was swimming back around towards the prow. As it got nearer him, Jack could feel his strength draining away. His legs started to feel like they were going to crumple underneath him at any moment, and he was struggling to keep his eyes open.

Arkus sensed him slipping away. *Keep moving, Jack,* he said. The words jolted Jack back to life. He swung the end of the rope up, and released it into the air. "Grab it!" he gasped.

Jack only succeeded in throwing it a little way above his head, but Arkus was ready for it, swooping down and snatching it out of the air in his teeth. He flew out over the side of the boat, the rope rapidly uncoiling behind him. Making a tight turn, he flew back towards the prow. Jack was teetering from side to side, looking as if he might collapse at any moment.

Jack, catch the rope.

The rope struck Jack squarely in the chest as Arkus flew over him, and he caught it, clinging on for his life with both hands, as Arkus flew up and away from the boat. As they climbed higher Jack felt his strength returning, and he started up the rope. When he'd climbed high enough, Arkus swung his head from side to side, and flipped him up on to his back.

"Thanks," puffed Jack, taking hold of his fur.

Jack let go of his part of the rope, and Arkus quickly took up the slack, pulling steadily. The *Blue Angel* below them swung around and followed, slicing through the water.

They were some distance from the coast when Jack felt an urgent call from Arkus. *Something is wrong! The rope is fighting me!*

Jack looked down at the *Blue Angel*. It was sitting at an angle in the water, its prow pointing sideways, creating a large wave down one side of its hull. At first he couldn't see what was causing this, but then he spotted a dark circular patch in the water a little way off, to one side. He stared harder, trying to work out what it was. The water inside it was swirling around, and he could see a faint red line around the outside. It was the Torg.

"It's making a whirlpool!" shouted Jack. "The boat's being sucked towards it."

The whirlpool continued to grow, becoming more powerful. Arkus flapped his wings harder trying to haul the boat away from it, but the pull on the rope was too much for him. The boat soon reached the edge of the whirlpool and was quickly drawn inside, swirling around and looking perilously close to capsizing. Arkus was being dragged around with it and was doing his best to keep them upright as the rope twisted, turning them upside down one minute, and then the right way up the next. As it went faster, they were pulled down ever closer to the spiralling and churning sea below. The spray was being whipped up into the air, drenching them.

Jack clung on tightly, wrapping his arms and legs around Arkus' neck. He could hardly feel his hands, which were aching with the cold, and he didn't know how much longer he could hold on. A gaping hole opened up in the centre of the whirlpool, threatening to swallow them down and take them to the bottom.

The boat had almost reached the edge of the hole when the whirlpool slowed.

The rope feels different, said Arkus.

Jack swept away wet hair from in front of his eyes, and looked down. The whirlpool had lost its ferocity, spinning more slowly, and the *Blue Angel* was settling back down into the water. He scoured the sea for the Torg, and spotted it swimming towards the beach.

"The Torg's heading back towards land," he said.

Arkus spoke to Kerra and Ryan. *Careful, it is coming back towards you.* There was a pause, then: *Jack, what is it I taste in the water?*

"Taste?" queried Jack.

Yes, in the spray from the ocean.

"Oh, that's salt," replied Jack.

There was a moan from on board the *Blue Angel*, and Cadan staggered out of the wheelhouse, rubbing the back of his neck. He stood staring at the prow and saw the rope mysteriously hanging down from the sky.

"Quick," said Jack. "Drop the rope."

Arkus opened his mouth, and the rope fell to

the deck. Cadan walked over to it and picked up the end, which still had Jack's oversized knot in it. He looked at it, then looked back up to where he'd seen it in the sky and shook his head, looking confused.

He dropped the rope and walked down the boat. The other members of the crew were also recovering, and he chatted to them, helping them to their feet on his way and then returning to the wheelhouse. The engine spluttered into life, and the *Blue Angel* swung around and headed back to port.

19

The Torg was now squatting on the beach just above the water line, the bumps on its back dull and barely glowing. Arkus and Jack had rejoined Kerra and Ryan on top of the promontory, and were looking down on top of it.

"It looks different," said Jack, "the bumps on it aren't as bright as before."

I believe it was troubled by the salt in the water, said Arkus. *I also found it unpleasant. We do not have this salt in our oceans.*

The Torg stirred, shuffled forwards, and then disappeared into the sand.

"It didn't take long to recover," said Ryan.

Come on, we must not lose it, said Arkus.

The Torg made its way inland, heading in the direction of the crater. It was moving very slowly, pausing every now and again as if exhausted. On reaching Oak Field, it moved uphill, and then stopped at the edge of the crater. Arkus came down a little further around, and then spoke.

Jack, you noticed something about the Torg when we were out there. What was it?

"It was when it was circling the boat," said Jack. "The bumps were really bright and flickering, creating red bands that seemed to move down its body."

"I saw that the other day," said Kerra, "when it was underneath those cables. It was flickering."

"Of course!" cried Jack, excitedly. "That must be it!"

"What is?" asked Kerra.

"When we saw it underneath those high voltage cables, we assumed it was using them to shield itself. But what if it was feeding?"

"Feeding - feeding on what?" asked Kerra.

"Feeding on the electricity passing through the cables," said Jack.

That might explain why it developed so fast, said Arkus.

"Well that's all very well, but I don't see how it helps us," said Ryan. "There's no high voltage cables round here."

"True," said Jack, "but I have another idea."

***

Arkus touched down gently in the middle of the back lawn. Jack saw the top kitchen window had been left ajar. He would need a leg up to reach it, but it would be easier than climbing all the way back up to his own window.

He turned to Ryan. "They've left the kitchen window open, could you give me a leg up?"

"Yeah, sure."

Jack and Ryan got down from Arkus and crept over to the window. Ryan gave Jack a leg up, and he clambered up on to the window-sill. Then, holding on to the edge of the top window to stop himself from falling, he reached inside with his other hand, pushed down the handle on the side window, and swung it open. He knew the key ought to be in the drawer under this window. Placing one hand on the draining board, he leaned inside and slid open the drawer. After a brief rummage around he found the key, with its distinctive wooden boat-shaped tag. He climbed back out, pushing the window closed behind him.

"Are you sure the Torg will be interested in the Zapper?" said Ryan as they walked down the garden. "It didn't seem very powerful to me."

"Oh, it's a bit different from when you last saw it. It's got a bigger motor now. The bolts of electricity it generates now are huge, they're like... like lightning."

Jack took the key from his pocket and unlocked the workshop door. The Zapper was sitting at the far end of the bench, and didn't have its dust cover on. That was good, thought Jack – it meant Uncle Fred hadn't got around to altering the motor speed. The battery was sitting on the bench underneath the end window, still wired up to the flagpole circuit. Jack unclipped the red and black crocodile clips, and then slid the battery to the edge of the bench, where he could get his fingers underneath it. He turned to Ryan.

"We'll need the rope. It should be on the back of the door?"

"Got it," said Ryan, throwing it over his shoulder.

They carried the battery and rope down the workshop to the Zapper, where Jack fixed the battery in place, pulling the straps down hard over the top of it so that it wouldn't fall off.

"Okay, it's ready. There should be some handles on the base at your side. Got them?"

"Yeah."

"OK... ready... lift!"

They carried the Zapper down the workshop

and out of the door. Jack pushed the door closed with his elbow, then, balancing the Zapper on one knee, he slid the key out from his pocket. He was about to put the key in the keyhole when a cloud shielded the moon.

"Great, now I can't see the lock," said Jack.

"Can't you feel around for it?"

"I can't do it with one hand, and if I let go with the other hand I'll drop the Zapper."

"We'll just have to leave it unlocked," said Ryan.

"We can't, someone might take everything," said Jack. He looked up at the large dark cloud making its way slowly across the moon. "We'll have to wait for that cloud to shift."

After a minute the cloud had moved away, and they were bathed in moonlight again. Jack located the keyhole, inserted the key and turned it. "Okay, it's locked now."

The Zapper was heavy, and it seemed to be getting heavier with each step, so they were relieved to get back to Arkus. He peered down at it as they lowered it down onto the grass at the side of him. *So, this is the machine you were thinking of. It's very small.*

"Er, yes," replied Jack, who didn't think it was small at all. They uncoiled the rope and fed the ends through the brass handles at one side of the Zapper, passing it underneath, and through the handles at the other side. Arkus lowered his head, so that they could slip the loop formed on one side of the Zapper over it. Then they took the ends of the rope protruding from the handles on the other side, and tied them around his middle.

Once they were happy it was all secure, they remounted Arkus. As Jack was shuffling along his back, he happened to glance up at the house, and was horrified to see Uncle Fred standing at one of the upstairs windows. He was staring down at the lawn. He opened the window, and pushed it back as far as it would go.

"It's sitting in the middle of the lawn, I tell you!" he shouted back to Aunt Lori in a slightly irritated raised voice. "Get out of bed and come and have a look if you don't believe me."

"The Zapper – he can see it!" hissed Jack.

Do not worry, it will become invisible once we are in the air, said Arkus.

Jack had seen enough. "OK, we're ready."

They took to the air. The slack in the rope was used up, and the Zapper lifted off the lawn, swinging gently from side beneath them.

20

When they arrived at the crater the Torg was sitting where they had left it. It didn't seem to have moved at all since it had returned from the beach.

"Can you place the Zapper down next to that tree near the middle of the crater?" said Jack.

I will try, replied Arkus.

He came down slowly, resting the Zapper gently on the ground before landing next to it. The three of them jumped down.

It was the first time Kerra had seen the

Zapper. "Is that a Van der Graaff Generator? We used one of those at school."

"Not like this one," said Jack.

"What do you mean?"

"You'll see," said Jack.

Arkus pressed his armband to make himself visible, and they removed the ropes from him. He told them he was going to check on the ship, and then set off towards the bush where they'd left it. Jack could hear a sadness in his voice, and knew he would be thinking about his home planet, a planet he would never see again.

After watching him go, they turned towards the tree.

"We need to find a place to hang it from," said Jack. "We'll need two strong branches – about halfway up."

They looked over the tree, searching for the right place.

"What about that branch there?" said Kerra, pointing to a sturdy looking branch on one side.

"Yeah, that'll do," said Jack.

"That one across from it looks good too," said Ryan.

"Great," said Jack. "All we've got to do now is get the ropes around them."

The branches were about halfway up, and perfectly placed. They lifted the Zapper over to the tree, placing it on the ground near the trunk. Jack took the two ends from one side, tied them around his waist, and then began to scale the tree. Sitting astride one of the branches they'd chosen, he undid the rope from around his waist, passed it around the branch and tied the ends together. He then shuffled back towards the trunk and climbed out on to the other branch before calling down to Ryan.

"Can you climb up here and hand me the loop from the other side?"

"You mean this bit?" said Ryan, pointing to the rope on the other side of the Zapper.

"Yes, that's it."

I think it would be easier for me to do that,

said Arkus, returning from his ship. *But be quick, I need to keep an eye on the Torg.* He picked the loop up in his mouth, and then swung around and passed it to Jack. As Jack took hold of it, he realised that he wouldn't be able to get the loop where he wanted it without removing the branches down each side. He now wished he'd brought a knife so that he could cut the loop in two.

I can bite through that, said Arkus, opening his mouth to reveal rows of razor-sharp teeth. It was the first time Jack had been so close to Arkus' teeth, and he found it a bit unnerving. He almost felt sorry for the Torg, knowing that if his plan worked, it would soon be torn apart by those teeth. He passed the rope back to Arkus. As he took his hand away, he heard a crunch.

There – take it.

Jack took the ends from Arkus. The rope had been sliced through at an angle, and the fibres it was made from were beginning to unravel. He took one end and passed it around the branch he was sitting on, and then tied the two ends in an untidy knot.

The Zapper was now sitting on the ground between the two branches, with the ropes travelling up from the handles at each side knotted around each branch. The only place Jack had ever seen it was in the workshop, and it was strange seeing it down on the ground below.

Arkus was standing nearby looking at his arm band. He was keeping a wary eye on the Torg, which seemed to be unaware of their presence.

I will attack from the top of the crater, said Arkus, taking to the air. He circled once around the crater before settling down at the top, just across from the Torg.

Jack climbed back down, joining Ryan and Kerra at the bottom of the tree. "There, that should do it. You two had better climb up there now. I'll power this up and then join you." He uncoiled the wires from the Zapper and connected them up to the battery. Then he called up to Ryan. "Stay near one of the loops, we'll need to raise it when the Torg comes."

He bent down, flicked the power switch to 'ON', and then swiftly climbed back up into the tree. Ryan was sitting astride one of the roped branches. Kerra had decided to go higher and was near the top, keeping look out. Jack made his way over to the other branch and sat down, his legs dangling down at each side. The knot he'd made was already coming undone, so he pulled on the frayed ends to re-tighten it. The whine of the motor on the Zapper got louder as its speed steadily increased, the belt inside the plastic tube becoming a blur.

Kerra called down. "Is that thing okay?"

Jack didn't have time to reply, as at that moment a bright white bolt of electricity leapt from the sphere down to the motor at the bottom of the tube, lighting up the ground around it. The motor speeded up, the whine becoming a high-pitched squeal.

The Torg is moving your way, said Arkus.

Jack shouted across to Ryan, "Quick, grab the rope, we need to raise it."

They pulled on the loops, raising it up off the ground.

"Hold it there!" shouted Jack, after they had raised it to waist height.

Just then the Torg appeared at the bottom of the tree. The bumps on its back brightened and flickered as it fed from the energy of the Zapper, but it was not coming up out of the ground.

"We need to raise it up more!" hollered Jack, trying to make himself heard above the noise of the motor, which was now generating an extremely loud high-pitched screech. It sounded as if it would fly apart at any moment.

They hauled on the ropes, raising the Zapper up higher still. The air around it was highly charged and fizzing, and Jack could feel the hairs on his arms lifting.

The front half of the Torg emerged from the ground, reaching up to the Zapper.

"It's working!" shouted Jack.

The Torg became more elongated, wavering from side to side, searching out the source of the energy. There was an almighty crack as a bolt leapt down from the sphere, striking it between the eyes. The Torg shook violently as a chain of bolts travelled down its body, leaping from bump to bump, then a stream of flame shot from the middle of its back up to the sphere. The flame enveloped the sphere, leaving a fiery violet ring around it. The Torg fell to the ground, thrashing about and screeching, as if it was in pain. The bumps on its back shrank away to nothing. Cracks began to appear across its body, splitting the Torg into narrow segments. The segments began to move, separating and wiggling away from one another, a green glow appearing at the end of each one.

"I think it's changing back into Ky," shouted Jack.

The violet flame swirled around the sphere, burning more and more ferociously. All of a sudden, a stream of flame broke free, flying upwards and striking Jack's ankle. Jack felt as if he'd been stung by several bees all at once and cried out in pain, letting go of the rope. The rope fell from his hands and was pulled down hard against the branch, jerking the knot undone. The Zapper swung down from the tree and the sphere fell off, bouncing and exploding in flame each time it met with the ground. There was a huge flash, and Jack was blinded for a second. When he looked back there was a trail of burning grass, leading over to the bush where Arkus' spaceship lay. The bush was on fire, and Arkus, having abandoned his attack, was beating it with his tail, trying to put it out.

Ryan called across from the branch opposite. "Can I lower this now?"

"Yeah," replied Jack. "Slowly though."

The Ky were winding around one another in a large squirming ball. In the dark their glows looked like some weird air display. They seemed oblivious to the Zapper as it came down to rest on the ground beside them.

Jack lifted his foot up onto the branch and rolled down his sock to inspect his ankle. There was a bright red mark where the flame from the sphere had struck.

Kerra climbed down and shuffled along the branch to join him. "That looks sore."

"Nah, it's all right," said Jack, trying to look brave, even though it was still hurting. He carefully pulled his sock back up over it.

"So these are the worms you saw?" asked Kerra, looking down at the Ky squirming on the ground below.

"Yeah. They seem so innocent, don't they? But you saw what they become."

21

They climbed down from the tree carefully avoiding the Ky, which were still massed together in a writhing ball. Jack flicked off the power on the Zapper, and the motor whined to a rest.

Arkus came back, having successfully extinguished all the fires, and they walked over to meet him. *The sphere from your machine caused a lot of damage.* He looked over towards the Ky. *The question now, is what do we do with...* He broke off, twisting his head around towards the fire-scorched bush. There was a pale blue light to one side. The light brightened, and then came towards them, stopping at the side of Arkus.

My ship! cried Arkus, looking fondly down at the small disc-shaped craft. The ship was humming and casting a pulsating blue ring on the ground beneath it.

It is operational, said Arkus, his voice breaking up with emotion. *And I am in contact with Falon once more.*

Kerra leant over towards Jack and whispered into his ear, "Who's Falon?"

"The ship's computer," whispered Jack. "It runs everything on board."

Falon has informed me that the Garner Ray is operational, stated Arkus. *The Ky will soon be secured in their cells.*

The spaceship rose into the air and flew over to the tree. It came to a standstill above the Ky, and emitted an orange beam. The beam struck one of the Ky, which immediately froze. Then the beam split into a multitude of smaller beams, covering the Ky's body in tiny orange dots, and the Ky started to shrink. As it became smaller the dots moved closer together. The Ky carried on shrinking until it was just a few inches long. Then, passing through the other Ky, who were still moving, it drifted up inside the beams into the bottom of the spaceship. Jack, Ryan and Kerra watched spellbound as the beam shrank each Ky and transferred it up to the spaceship.

As they were watching the last of the Ky disappear, someone yelled out from the top of the crater. "Who's down there?"

It was a voice they recognised. The voice of PC Harkin.

A powerful beam swept across the crater, passing the tree. It hovered over the grass to one side for a moment, and then moved back, shining directly on the Zapper.

"Right, I'm coming down there!" shouted PC Harkin. He started down the side of the crater, the beam from his torch sweeping from side to side in front of him as he picked out his way.

"Oh no, he's going to see the Zapper," said Jack.

Do not worry, said Arkus. *He will be dealt with.*

The ship moved across the crater towards PC Harkin, the flickering blue lights from its engines spreading out across the ground. PC Harkin had reached the bottom of the crater, and saw it coming towards him. He shone his torch at it. "Who... who's there?" he called out nervously.

The ship flew higher, and then a broad orange beam appeared from underneath it. It extended down to envelop him, and he went limp.

"You're not going to shrink him too, are you?" asked Kerra.

No, that will not be necessary, replied Arkus.

The ship flew up, pulling PC Harkin off his feet. It was a strange sight. He appeared to be unconscious, his arms and legs dangling and his head lolling to one side. It went higher still, its strange cargo suspended beneath it, then flew over the rim of the crater and disappeared. A minute later it returned without the unfortunate police officer.

I have placed him at the bottom of the hill, said Arkus. *Now, we must get to work and return your machine.*

"Won't he just come back up here again?" asked Jack.

No, he will have been disorientated by the beam.

The rope to one side of the Zapper had slipped out from one of the handles, so Jack re-threaded it, pulling enough through to tie around Arkus. As he was doing this he noticed that the sphere was missing, and remembered what had happened to it.

"What is it?" asked Kerra, seeing the worried look on his face.

"I just remembered what happened to the sphere," said Jack. "I hope it's okay."

They walked over to the bush, following a line of burnt patches in the grass. The sphere was lying in the middle of another much larger burnt patch, close to where Arkus' ship had rested. The side of the bush which had concealed it had been burnt to a crisp. The sphere seemed to have lost its shine.

"It looks different," said Ryan.

"Maybe it got scorched by the fire," said Kerra.

Jack picked it up, and found it hot to the touch. It appeared to be covered in a layer of what looked like soot. "Come on, let's get out of here before Harkin comes back."

They fitted the sphere back on to the Zapper, and then tied the ropes around Arkus again.

I have asked Falon to fly the ship away from the crater, and then keep it on the ground until my return, said Arkus.

Once they were sitting astride him, Arkus pressed the band on his arm to make himself invisible, and took to the air. As they rose above the edge of the crater, they could see PC Harkin making his way back up the hill. Arkus swept around, swooping down low over the oak tree in the corner before landing behind the gate.

Kerra climbed down. "Is this the last time I'll see you?"

Yes, I'm afraid so, said Arkus.

"Oh, well. Goodbye then." said Kerra.

Goodbye, and thank you for your help.

She looked up in Jack's direction. "I usually go down to the beach around one. I might see you there sometime."

"Eh... yeah, right," said Jack.

"Bye then. Safe journey, Arkus."

Arkus took to the air again. As they went higher, Jack spotted PC Harkin down in the crater, shining his torch on the half-burnt bush.

"He's got a puzzle on his hands," said Jack.

"Yeah," said Ryan. "You wait till he finds that strange goo on the rocks."

22

The house was quiet as they landed in the middle of the back lawn. Jack was relieved to see all the lights were out, which probably meant he hadn't been missed. They jumped down, untied the Zapper and carried it to the workshop, placing it down at the far end of the bench in the same spot it had occupied before. After locking the door, they walked back to Arkus.

"So, this is goodbye" said Jack, staring up to where he imagined Arkus's head to be.

Yes, I'm afraid I must return to my people,

said Arkus. *But I must thank you for all your help. I could not have done it without you.*

"Goodbye then," said Jack.

"Bye," said Ryan.

Arkus flapped his wings. The cool night air swirled about them, and then he was gone.

"Do you think we'll be able to see his ship take off from here?" asked Ryan.

"We might," said Jack. "We'll probably see it better from the bottom of the garden."

Passing the workshop, they followed the narrow concrete path down the side of the vegetable patch, and then stood with their elbows on top of the wooden fence at the bottom, looking out over the large field beyond. A new day was dawning, the sky above it gradually turning pale grey. They didn't have long to wait before they saw a blue spot drift up into the air behind the crater.

"There it is!" cried Ryan.

The spot brightened and became a thin blue line arcing across the sky like the top edge of a rainbow and sweeping around towards them. It hovered a short distance away over the field.

Arkus spoke to them for the last time. *Goodbye my friends.* Then in a flash it shot up into the sky and disappeared into a cloud, leaving a vivid blue trail behind it.

"Wow!" said Jack. "Who'd have thought that tiny spaceship could move so fast."

"Yeah," said Ryan. "That was amazing."

***

"Can you give me a leg up?" said Jack, who was now standing in front of the kitchen window. The top window was where he'd left it, so it was an easy job to reach in and open the side window again.

"See you tomorrow then," whispered Jack.

"Yeah, see you," said Ryan. "It won't be early. I think I'll have a bit of a lie in."

"Yeah, me too," said Jack.

He closed the window quietly behind him and slipped down off the side, landing softly on his feet. After returning the key to the drawer, where Uncle Fred would expect to find it, he crept upstairs to his room. Cody heard him coming in. He raised his head, looked up at him for a moment, stretched, and then curled up again. Jack undressed, climbed into bed, and was asleep almost as soon as his head hit the pillow.

23

Jack came downstairs still feeling half asleep, the night's adventure having taken its toll. His aunt and uncle were in the kitchen chatting over mugs of coffee.

"I was wondering when you were going to surface," said Aunt Lori, seeing him by the door. "I heard Cody scratching at your door a while back, so I let him out. You were sleeping so solidly I didn't wake you. We had breakfast a couple of hours ago. There's bread over there if you're hungry – I could toast it?"

"I'm not all that hungry," said Jack.

Uncle Fred got up from the table. "Not hungry eh? Well if you're not going to eat anything, I need to ask you about something."

Jack followed his uncle out of the back door and down the garden. Limping and favouring his good leg, Uncle Fred appeared to be in a hurry. As Jack scurried along behind him, he was wondering if he was in trouble, and if so, what it might be about. Uncle Fred went inside the workshop and walked to the far end, stopping at the side of the Zapper.

He pointed to the sphere on top. "There, look at that!"

Jack stared at it in disbelief. The sphere had been completely transformed. He'd thought last night that it had looked different, but he could never have imagined how different. The whole sphere was wrapped in flames. Intense pink flames surrounded the top. Then came petrol-blue flames, twisting and entwining with green. A fusion of yellow and orange flames circled the middle, with turquoise and then violet flames around the bottom.

The flames danced and shimmered, looking almost real.

"Isn't that something!" said Uncle Fred.

"Yeah, it's amazing," said Jack. His uncle didn't seem in the least bit upset. In fact he was clearly delighted.

"Do you think it was caused by those huge bolts the other day?" asked Uncle Fred, gazing at the sphere.

"Yeah, probably," said Jack.

He spotted a lump of mud with blades of grass sticking out of it under the corner of the base nearest him, and surreptitiously flicked it off with his finger.

"Can't understand why we didn't see it," said Uncle Fred, who was beginning to ramble to himself. "Under a layer of this strange black stuff... Burnt right into the metal somehow... Doesn't rub off... You know, it's strange, but I thought I saw the Zapper last night. It was just sitting in the middle of the ..."

"Maybe we ought to replace it," butted in Jack. He was trying to stop his uncle thinking about seeing the Zapper.

Uncle Fred turned towards him. "What was that?"

"The sphere – do you think we ought to replace it? I mean, it's not silver any more."

"Oh, no, I quite like it. Although I think I might have to make another one later on. Your aunt has her eye on this one – she thinks it will make a lovely flowerpot."

Jack gave a secret smile of relief. It looked as if their crazy adventure would remain a secret after all.

Also available by Martin Berry and published by Mereo,
THE SAPPHIRE CRYSTAL

BV - #0092 - 220922 - C0 - 203/127/13 - PB - 9781861519566 - Gloss Lamination